THE BERRYFIELDS OF BLAIR

Following the loss of her son William in World War I, and the subsequent death of her husband, Betsy Meldrum tries to make a success of the family farm, helped by her daughters Marian and Elspeth. Eventually, however, she has to sell the farm and Marian becomes a teacher at the local school, but her relationship with the new owner, Paul Holt, gets off to a bad start. As Paul tries to make a success of the berry farm, the Meldrums begin to adjust to their new life, until a stranger arrives from France with startling news...

THE BERRYFIELDS OF BLAIR

The Berryfields Of Blair

by

Anne Forsyth

Magna Large Print Books
Long Preston, North Yorkshire,
BD23 4ND, England.

British Library Cataloguing in Publication Data.

Forsyth, Anne
    The berryfields of Blair.

    A catalogue record of this book is
    available from the British Library

    ISBN   0-7505-2375-1

First published in Great Britain by D. C. Thomson

Copyright © Anne Forsyth

Cover illustration © Len Thurston by arrangement with
P.W.A. International Ltd.

The moral right of the author has been asserted

Published in Large Print 2005 by arrangement with
Dorian Literary Agency

Magna Large Print is an imprint of Library Magna Books Ltd.

Printed and bound in Great Britain by
T.J. (International) Ltd., Cornwall, PL28 8RW

Chapter One

'I can't wait till Saturday!' Marian looked up from her sewing and smiled at her young sister.

'You're going to break that chair if you keep swinging on it like that, Elspeth.'

The girls' mother, Betsy, turned from the stove, and she and Marian exchanged a fond look.

Elspeth was such a child still, though she was in the first year at high school. And she couldn't hide her excitement about the local Fair o' Blair Day!

And why not, Marian thought, pausing to thread her needle. After the long years of war, it was time to look ahead.

She gave a wistful sigh, remembering her brother, William, who had gone off so cheerfully to the war and had fallen at the Somme.

Life had been hard for the Meldrum family after that. Their father, too, had passed away after a short illness, brought on, no doubt, by the news of the death of his son.

But now, here was Elspeth, growing up

into a lively girl, and over the moon with excitement about Fair o' Blair Day.

'This will be the first time it's been held since 1913,' Betsy said. 'There are sure to be big crowds in Skirmie Park.'

'You'll be there, won't you, Marian?' Elspeth begged her elder sister. 'You'll come and see me running in the Guides race?'

'Of course!' Marian laughed. 'It'll be a good day out.' She put down her darning mushroom. 'There, that's done! I'll never know how you wear such holes in your stockings,' she told her sister with a smile.

'It's time you learned to mend your own stockings,' her mother scolded. 'I'm sure I've shown you often enough.'

'I haven't time!' Elspeth said dramatically. 'There's such a lot to do – and I haven't even done my practice yet.'

'Well, you've time now, before your tea.' Betsy turned back to the stove.

'She's doing well,' Marian remarked, as Elspeth started practising scales on the piano. 'Miss Macfarlane was telling me she might put her in for the music festival. She hasn't told Elspeth yet, though.'

'Time enough,' Betsy agreed. 'No doubt she'll be in a right taking about it...'

There was a silence, as Marian folded up

8

the mending and put it away. The warm afternoon sunshine flooded the big farmhouse kitchen, and Marian looked affectionately round the room she had known and loved all her life.

Here she had curled up on the big settle in front of the range; here she had sat at the table and done her homework.

Pots of bright red geraniums stood on the window-sill, and when she looked out of the windows, she could see the Rhode Island Reds scratching on the gravel path and the ginger cat spread out on the low wall in the sun, sound asleep.

It was home, this old stone farmhouse, just outside Blairgowrie. Marian loved the green Perthshire landscape; the long, warm summers, the fields golden at harvest time – even the bare trees, black against the winter skyline.

She couldn't imagine living anywhere else.

'While she's out of the room,' Betsy said, trying to speak casually, 'have you got time to come to Dundee with me this week?'

'Why?' Marian looked surprised. 'What do you want to do?'

'I've had a letter from the lawyer,' her mother explained. She took it from behind the clock on the mantelpiece.

'Read it,' she said, handing the letter over. 'See if you can work out what he wants.'

'There's nothing to worry about,' Marian said comfortingly after scanning the contents for a few moments. 'It sounds to me as if it's just a matter of documents to sign, something like that. You know how careful Mr Jamieson is. He's a stickler for every little detail.'

'Well, I suppose that's his job,' her mother said resignedly. 'And he's guided us well all these years. Well, Marian, will you come with me?'

'Of course. And afterwards we can have a look round the shops and a cup of tea in one of the tearooms.' Marian smiled. 'Make a day of it.'

At last her mother seemed to relax.

'There was some crêpe de Chine advertised in Wilson's. I thought it might make up into a nice dress for you.'

'I wish *I* was better with a needle,' Marian said ruefully. 'I can manage this sort of thing...' She gestured offhandedly towards the pile of mending. 'But nothing fancy.'

'You do fine. You've many other talents that matter more.'

Marian glowed. Her mother wasn't one to praise lightly.

Betsy looked at her elder daughter with unreserved pride, at her unruly red-gold hair and fresh complexion, her ready smile... She'd given up her plans to teach, though she'd been trained, and had been willing to help on the farm when William enlisted.

And hadn't she kept things going, sometimes working alongside the hands, helping with the harvest and toiling all hours without complaint? With a tightening in her throat, Betsy remembered, too, how gently Marian coaxed her mother back to life in the terrible black days after William was killed in action.

If only her daughter could meet someone who was right for her, Betsy thought. Her proud, brave, beautiful girl deserved happiness, a home and family of her own...

Marian's heart was light when she set off for Skirmie Park.

She loved the little town she'd grown up in and where she knew so many folk.

People nodded and smiled at the tall girl in the blue cotton dress as she made her way to the entrance to the park.

'A fine lass, that!' one old farmer remarked to his companion. He'd known the family for years and admired the way Marian had coped during the war.

Betsy had decided to stay at home.

'You two go and enjoy yourselves,' she'd told her daughters. 'I'll have the tea ready for you when you come back.'

Marian wandered through the field on her own, enjoying the feeling of freedom and a day away from her usual chores.

It seemed everyone in the district had come along for the Games. There was a pipe band and dancers, a tug-o'-war, and a group of young men limbering up for tossing the caber...

'What a turnout,' a voice behind her said. 'Glad you could make it, Marian.'

'Robert!' She whirled round and looked up at the tall young man who stood smiling down at her. 'What are you doing here?'

'The same as you, enjoying a day out.' He laughed.

'I mean ... how can you get time off? That is...'

He gave that deep chuckle she remembered so well.

'There were no emergencies today, and if there are, my father will handle them.'

'I'm sure you've earned a break.'

Marian and Robert were old friends. She remembered him from their schooldays, a lanky, earnest boy whose one ambition was

12

to be a doctor.

She'd seen very little of him after he went off to university, but his father talked often of his son and how he'd be joining him in the practice 'one of these days'.

Now Robert was back in the countryside where he had grown up, and was as well respected by his patients as his father was.

'I was sorry to hear about your brother,' he said gently.

Marian nodded, feeling his sympathy. She knew Robert so well, there was no need for many words between them.

'You've been away, too, in the war. Were you in France?'

'Yes...' There was a pause. 'But I was one of the lucky ones ... I came back.

'You've not had such an easy time yourself, Marian. How's the farm? I hear you're a real working farmer!'

'It's Geordie and Bob who do most of the work,' Marian protested, 'not me.'

'I've heard differently.' He took her hand and looked down at it, work-hardened and rough.

Marian, embarrassed, snatched it away.

'Oh, we've managed,' she went on quickly. 'We've been fortunate. Last year, the floods...'

'I remember,' he mused. 'I'd just been demobilised. The Ericht broke its banks and the stubble fields were flooded.'

She nodded.

'We didn't escape completely, but we were luckier than some. And we've put a couple of acres down to rasps. It'll be easier to get help now the men are coming back from the war... Oh, I've great plans.'

She broke off suddenly at a flurry of activity at the edge of the field.

'It's the Girl Guide races now, Robert. Elspeth will never forgive me if I miss it!'

'I'll come, too, if you'll let me...'

Robert took her arm, and for a moment Marian allowed herself to feel how pleasant it was to be escorted, to have someone looking after her, steering her gently through the crowds.

'There she is!'

As Marian smiled and waved enthusiastically to her young sister, Robert thought how attractive she looked with the breeze rustling through her hair, her blue eyes sparkling.

'Will you let me take you both home afterwards?' he asked. 'I've got the car here.'

'What a treat! I haven't been in a car for a long time. Neither has Elspeth.'

'Then it'll be a pleasure to drive you both.'

14

'Here they come!'

Marian turned to watch the race and Robert, for her sake, tried to share her enthusiasm. But his eyes were on the girl at his side and how she'd changed. He remembered Marian as a scrawny, impetuous schoolgirl.

Marian clapped her hands in delight when her sister passed the finishing line.

'Did you see it? I came in second!' Elspeth danced up to them, almost tripping in her enthusiasm.

'Well done, Elspeth.' Robert smiled at her. 'It's hard work, running races. Would you like some tea or lemonade, and cakes? I expect you're hungry.'

'Yes, I am.' Elspeth beamed.

It was a day to remember, Marian thought as they walked the length of the field together. Enjoying the sunshine and the races and the band playing – it all seemed miles away from the farm, and the nagging worries about money and the uncertainty of the harvest.

'This is kind of you,' she told Robert. 'It's nice to be spoiled – sometimes.'

'Marian, I wish…' he began, but then stopped. It was too soon. This wasn't the time or place…

'A cup of tea, then?' he suggested brightly.

'And lemonade for you, Elspeth? I believe you've earned it!'

Next morning, Marian woke early, aware that something was happening that day.

The visit to the lawyer in Dundee – that was it. She dressed quickly, eager to get the morning chores out of the way. But when she went downstairs, she found her mother sitting at the kitchen table, a cup of tea in front of her. Her face was white and drawn.

'Are you all right?' Marian was concerned. It was so unlike Betsy to sit down, especially first thing in the morning.

Betsy turned towards her daughter.

'I've one of my bad headaches, dear,' she explained.

Marian was instantly sympathetic.

'You go right back upstairs and lie down. I'll see to the hens, and make the breakfast. You shouldn't have risen at all.'

'But the lawyer...' Betsy protested weakly.

'Never mind about that. I can go on my own,' Marian said cheerfully.

'Would you, dear? I don't think I could manage today...'

'Come on,' Marian urged her. 'Back upstairs to bed. I'll draw the curtains and you'll have peace and quiet.'

16

Her mother didn't protest.

'You're a great help to me, Marian. I don't know what I'd do without you...'

Early in the afternoon, Marian set off for the train. It was another fine day, so she decided to walk across the fields to Coupar Angus station, to catch the Dundee train.

Elspeth was spending the day with a school friend, and Betsy was resting comfortably. Though Marian felt a wave of sympathy for her mother – these headaches often left her feeling limp and weak – she was still looking forward to her afternoon in Dundee.

It seemed a long time since she'd visited the city and her spirits lifted at the thought of a day's window-shopping and a nice pot of tea afterwards.

On the way to the lawyer's office, she stopped to admire a blouse in ivory jap silk in Draffen's window. There was a fashionable hat with tassels, too. And the dresses! How elegant the designs were, in crêpe de Chine and tussore... Marian gazed in admiration, almost forgetting the purpose of her visit.

Then she shook herself, realising she mustn't be late. She promised herself she'd spend more time in the shops on the way home.

She made her way to the office, and Mr Jamieson's secretary showed her into the familiar room with its high ceiling and book-lined shelves.

From the window you could look out over the docks. Marian had always enjoyed this view. She liked to see the DP&L steamers about to sail from Dundee to Newcastle, Hull and on to London and fancy that, one day, she might board a ship and set off on a voyage.

'Miss Marian, it's good to see you, as always,' Mr Jamieson greeted her.

'My mother has a bad headache,' Marian explained. 'So I'm here in her place.'

'Ah, I see. I'm sorry to hear Mrs Meldrum's not well … I hope she'll soon be better.' There was a little pause. 'I wonder, would you like a cup of tea?'

'No, thank you.' Marian shook her head.

'Well, in that case, we should begin…'

The lawyer had known Marian since she was a pigtailed schoolgirl, all arms and legs, and had seen her grow up. He had admired the way she had coped without complaint, all through the war. He paused, wondering how she would take the news.

'How are things going?' he asked, to give himself a little time.

'Quite well.' Marian sat, looking composed, her hands folded in her lap. 'The harvest should be better this year, and I hope we'll do well with the rasps. We're not on the same scale as the big farms, yet, of course. But we'll take on pickers from Dundee...'

How he wished he had better news to give her.

'Miss Marian,' he began, giving a little cough, 'I'm afraid the news I have for you is not – encouraging.'

Marian looked at him steadily.

'It's about money, isn't it?'

'Yes. There isn't enough coming in, and the capital ... well, there's very little of that left. Certainly not enough to keep the farm going.'

'But, now that the men are coming back from the war,' the girl said eagerly, 'we'll be able to employ someone to help Geordie and Bob. Maybe even a farm manager to oversee things – the job my ... my brother would have done.'

She hurried on, afraid of breaking down.

'Do you think, is it possible ... a bank loan, perhaps, to tide us over...?'

He shook his head.

'I'm afraid not. I've looked at every option but there aren't enough funds to carry out repairs or employ staff…'

'So, what you're telling me…' Marian tried to keep her voice steady.

'The farm must be sold,' he interrupted softly.

There was a silence. Marian hardly heard the lawyer as he showed her the figures and explained the deficit.

'You wouldn't be without a home,' he said kindly. 'I understand there's a cottage on the farm?'

Marian nodded dumbly.

'I think the farm would fetch a good price,' he continued. 'I'll look out for a possible buyer, if you like.'

'That would be kind.' Marian spoke automatically, her mind in turmoil. There was so much to think about.

'What about Geordie and Bob?' she said at last. 'Geordie's been with us for years and now his son, Bob. And Jess, Geordie's wife, comes to help in the house sometimes. We couldn't see them turned away…'

'I can't speak for a new employer,' Mr Jamieson said carefully, 'but I'll certainly do what I can.'

'Thank you.' Marian rose to go.

'I with it were better news,' he said gently.

She made her way, unseeing, downstairs

and out into the streets. She had little heart for window-shopping now, and didn't want to stop at her favourite tearoom. Her appetite had gone completely.

On the way home, she looked out blankly at the countryside and wondered how she would break the shattering news to Betsy and Elspeth.

As she walked along the lane towards the farmhouse in the early evening sunshine, she thought the house had never looked more beautiful.

Honeysuckle clambered over the old stone wall; there was the Marechal Niel rose, and the old Jacobite rose that her father had planted in the year of Elspeth's birth.

It was home, it was where she belonged. But, soon, it wouldn't be home any longer.

She couldn't put off telling her mother and sister. They would be able to see something was wrong immediately.

Betsy was dozing lightly in her favourite chair, while Elspeth was reading, perched on a cushion in the window alcove.

'Hello!' Elspeth sprang up, letting her book fall to the floor. 'Did you have a good time? Did you buy anything? I bet you did. I bet you liked *everything!*'

Marian smiled weakly.

'Are you feeling better, Mother?' she asked, turning to Betsy, who was still looking a little wan. 'You shouldn't be up.'

'I'm much better, dear. Did you have a nice time in Dundee? What did Mr Jamieson want?'

Marian drew a deep breath.

'I have news for you both. Yes, Elspeth, you, too.' She paused. 'But I'm afraid it's bad news...'

'That was a very fine dinner, my dear, very fine indeed.'

Laurence Holt dabbed his mouth with his napkin as he looked approvingly round the dining-room.

What he saw there always gave him pleasure – the red plush chairs, heavily carved mahogany sideboard and dining-table. The velvet drapes perfectly framed the windows, and the well-chosen landscapes complemented the wallpaper.

He appreciated his surroundings all the more because it was all the result of his own hard work.

Sometimes, he would remind his wife and family that they owed this comfort to his struggles, right from the early days.

'Born in the back streets of Salford,' he

would say. 'We had cast-off boots for Sundays, but otherwise, we went barefoot...'

'Oh, Father, not *that* again!' Sarah, his daughter, would protest. 'We've heard it all before...'

'Don't be impertinent to your father,' Grace, his wife, would put in hastily. Sarah was a pleasure to them both – slim, lively, with dark curls and bright eyes. But she had strong views, and she seemed to take pleasure in teasing her father, provoking him with her radical ideas.

Paul, their son, was different, Laurence thought proudly. Sensible and level-headed. Look how well he'd done in the war. Oh, it had been an anxious time, with him away at the Front, but he was safely home again now.

It was time to put all that behind him. Look to the future... Laurence glanced across the room at Grace.

She'd done well, too, never complaining, though she was often anxious. Laurence knew he wasn't the easiest of men to live with.

'We'll have our coffee in the drawing-room.' Grace nodded to the maid who came to clear away.

'A nice piece of beef, that,' Laurence remarked.

'I'll be sure to tell Cook.' Grace rose and led the way into the drawing-room.

Laurence smiled to himself. He never failed to enjoy this little ceremony. A *drawing-room!* Time was, he'd lived in one room and a kitchen, with his mother and brothers and sisters. There had been seven of them. And now, look at all this!

'Are the children out tonight?' he asked, picking up the newspaper.

'Sarah's with some of her artist friends at a meeting at the Free Trade Hall.'

Laurence rustled the pages of his paper angrily.

'I wish she'd make more suitable friends,' he grumbled. 'It's time she met a nice young man and settled down. It's not fitting for a girl from a good family to be so … forward!'

'She's young yet,' Grace, always the peacemaker, soothed. 'There's plenty of time, dear.'

'I don't like it. She's far too opinionated – for a girl!'

'Paul will be in soon,' Grace said brightly, trying to distract him.

Her husband's face cleared. He was proud of his only son. There was never any trouble with Paul. He'd be a real credit to the family.

'That sounds like him now,' Grace looked

up. 'I'd better see about some dinner for him.'

Laurence folded the newspaper and laid it down as his son strode into the room.

'It's a fine night out,' he greeted the young man.

'Is it? I hadn't noticed.' Paul sat down heavily in a chair by the door.

His father glanced at him. He looked a little upset, not his usual self. Except ... Paul hadn't really been his usual self for a while. Edgy, inclined to snap ... well, it was only to be expected.

The boy – his father still thought of him as a boy – had had a difficult time. All those months in the trenches in France must have left their mark. Paul never spoke of it. He hadn't even mentioned the award he'd received for bravery in the field.

Laurence filled his pipe slowly, waiting for Paul to speak.

'Your mother's gone to see to a bit of dinner for you,' he said at last. 'She always thinks you'll starve if you miss a meal.'

He smiled, inviting his son to join in his amusement.

'She needn't trouble,' Paul replied dully. 'I'm not hungry.'

'It's kindly meant,' Laurence put in. Then,

as the silence continued, he assumed his usual serious expression.

'I've been talking to Manson...'

'Manson?'

'At the works, you know...'

'Of course. Your manager.'

Laurence nodded.

'Now that you're back and settled in, we thought you could start off with a couple of months in the factory, just to get into the way of things. Not that much has changed ... we've not invested a lot in the past few years. With the war...'

'Ah, yes.' Paul rose and took a cigarette from the silver box on the mantelpiece. 'The war...'

'Then, of course, you'll have your own ideas – about expansion, I mean. After all, the war's over. We've got to look to the future, and I can see bright prospects for us in the States...' His father looked thoughtful before continuing.

'Maybe you could go on a tour of America, looking at factories there, say in a year or two.'

'Father.' Paul turned. At over six feet, he was very much the taller man.

Laurence looked up at him approvingly. Paul had the looks, no doubt about that.

Where did he get the fair hair, the clear gaze, the lithe, energetic build? Nothing like me, Laurence thought proudly. But in other ways – just like me! Straight as a die, honest, good with the men. He'll make a grand job of the business. Holt and Son...

He forced himself back to the present.

'Well, what do you think?'

'Father,' Paul said again. 'There's something I want to say.'

'Out with it, lad. If you've new ideas, let's hear them! That's what we want – new blood, new thinking. In the business world, you can't stand still.'

'It's not that... I've got to think it over. I mean...' Suddenly, his son was shaking. He got up, and stubbed the cigarette out in a cut-glass dish. 'Excuse me, Father!'

Laurence gazed at his son as Paul slammed out of the room.

'Your dinner's in the dining...' Grace stood in astonishment as her son nearly collided with her in his haste to escape.

'Whatever's the matter with Paul?' she demanded. 'Have you had an argument? Laurence, is something wrong?'

'Of course not.' Her husband was bewildered. 'I can't imagine what's got into the boy. One moment he was right as rain, then

27

he rushed out of the room...'

'I expect it's a girl,' his wife said comfortably. 'He's maybe upset about her ... whoever she may be.'

'Nonsense,' Laurence said sharply. 'We were speaking about the factory.'

'I'll go up and see if he wants anything to eat...'

'Best leave him, Grace,' her husband advised.

Upstairs, Paul sat in his room, fists clenched. In his mind he could hear the relentless hiss and stamp of the machines, the deafening sound of grinding filling the whole factory. Like the guns, he thought, those damned guns! Day and night ... never stopping for a moment...

He rose and, controlling his feelings with an effort, stood by the window, looking down into the quiet tree-lined street.

He didn't know how long he stood there. There was a light tap at the door, and he ignored it. Another knock. He sighed.

'Come in.'

The relief on his face as he turned was visible.

'Oh, I'm glad it's you.'

'Did you think it would be Mother or Father?'

His sister, still wearing her cloak, stood there, looking amused.

'Well,' he said, 'I'd rather it was you.'

'They're in a right taking downstairs, you know.' Sarah flung herself into a chair. 'Father's upset because you stormed out and Mother's fretting because you didn't want your dinner.'

He groaned.

'I'd better apologise, then, I suppose.'

'I don't see why.' Sarah's dark eyes were full of compassion. 'Can you tell *me* what's the matter? As if I didn't know.'

'Then I needn't explain.'

'You don't want to go into the factory.'

'Is it as clear as that?' he asked.

'It is to me.'

'Oh, Sarah, I know I should have said something earlier. But Father takes it for granted that it's what I want – to succeed him...'

'And you don't want to,' her sister finished for him.

'I never did, really. But especially not now, since the war. It's the noise of the factory ... and the boredom.

'I suppose I'm lucky,' he went on, 'having the chance of a job when there are so many people unemployed. But, you see, I know

29

what I want to do.'

'That's wonderful!' Sarah jumped up. 'Then why not do it?'

'That's easily said.' He smiled at her, beginning to recover his spirits. 'Remember when I was in hospital, early on in the war? I was in a convalescent home in Perthshire, not far from a little town called Blairgowrie. I've always wanted to go back there, buy a farm, maybe, or a smallholding.'

'But – farming?' Sarah was puzzled. 'It's so different, Paul. You don't know much about it.'

'I worked on a farm, remember, in Galloway, before the war? All that time in the trenches, that was what kept me going. I thought, if I get through, that's what I'm going to do with my life. But Father's set his heart on my following him. I don't know how to tell him.'

'But how will you be able to afford it, Paul? Pa's not likely to want to lend you money, is he?'

'There's Aunt Maria's legacy. I haven't touched that.'

'Yes, the favourite nephew...' Sarah smiled without rancour. 'She left me her sapphires, and I'm not really the type who wears jewels.'

She looked down at her strong boots, and remembered where they'd taken her … on a protest march … into depressing homes in the poorer parts of the city … even a settlement in the slums.

'You'll have to tell him,' she said at last.

'I suppose so – the sooner the better.' He patted her shoulder. 'You and I, we can talk to each other. I've always been glad of that.'

She paused.

'So, have you decided when all this will begin?'

'I'll go up to Scotland, look around, see what's up for sale.'

He straightened up and Sarah saw again the elder brother she'd admired – the one who'd defended her when she was a child, who'd walked with her on that terrifying first day at school.

Paul wasn't afraid of anything, certainly not of facing their parents with the truth.

'They'll come round,' she said. 'Once they know it's what you really want to do.'

'I hope so.' Paul raised his chin in the gesture she knew so well. 'What better time than the present? I'm going to talk to Father – now.'

Marian put down her duster and opened

the window. She took a deep breath. Yes, it was definitely spring. There was a feeling in the air. She could see a clump of bright yellow crocuses and the catkins were budding down by the burn. Suddenly, she began to feel more hopeful. It had been a hard winter, the winter of 1921...

First, there had been storm damage early in December. The fields had been flooded, and the whole countryside had been similarly affected. Even in Dundee there had been unusually high tides which had ruined the jute sheds.

Then January brought the snow ploughs out. Blizzards and drifting snow had swept Perthshire and farmers were forced to hand-feed their sheep. Only Elspeth and her friends had enjoyed the harsh weather. There was tobogganing on the slopes and Elspeth would rush home every day, rosy-cheeked and smiling.

But gradually, the snow had melted. Betsy had enjoyed going out into the garden as the weather grew milder.

'Look what I've found,' she'd exclaim, pointing to the clump of purple hellebores or some shrub she thought she had lost. The winter jasmine made a brave show around the doorway, and in the dip at the end of the garden a carpet of snowdrops lifted the gloom.

Marian had worried about her mother. What a wrench it would be, leaving the old farmhouse, the home she'd come to as a bride. The family home with its big kitchen, its familiar parlour with her father's rolltop desk, and his chair. So many things her mother had loved... Now, it would all change.

But, although Betsy had been silent and preoccupied for a week or two, after a bit, she became philosophical.

'Well, we must get used to it,' she said briskly.

Marian watched her mother closely. Was she just putting a brave face on things for the sake of the family? She couldn't be sure.

Then, one winter evening, Marian sat reading by the fireside while her mother did some sewing. Outside, the wind was howling round the eaves, and sighing through the beech trees at the end of the garden.

Suddenly, the scullery door was blown open, and Marian rose to shut it.

'There's a proper draught in here,' she said. 'It's the small window – there's a crack in it. No wonder it's so cold.'

She secured the door and put a bolster

against the foot to keep the heat in, before adding another log to the fire.

Betsy held out her hands to the welcome blaze.

'Next winter we'll be snug enough,' she said. 'These draughts, that icy cold passage – it's a thought to rise and go to your bed at nights. I'll be glad to move.'

Marian stared at her mother, amazed. Betsy laid down her sewing and looked across at her daughter.

'You thought I'd be broken-hearted at the thought of moving? Well, I am sad, of course, in a way. This was our home – but it's not been the same without your father. And it's so cold and draughty in winter. This house needs a lot spent on it. Maybe the new owner will have the money to improve things. We certainly hadn't.'

She smiled at Marian's astonishment.

'So you see, I'll be glad to move. It's a fine little cottage we're going to. Your father had it all done up when he let it to the Macneil family.'

Marian remembered the Macneils from when Jim had worked on the farm. He and his wife had three lively boys who were always getting into trouble. But the cottage had stood empty since they left. It was time it was occupied.

'We could get one of those new gas grates,' Betsy said thoughtfully. 'Think how easy it would be. No more cleaning out the ashes and bringing in the coals!'

Soon, Marian found that she, too, was eagerly looking forward to the move. No more scrubbing the cold stone floor, no more laundering heavy curtains every year. No more washing down and distempering the scullery...

There would be work to do in the cottage, but it would be much easier to run. For the first time in years, Marian felt a sense of lightness.

During the past few months, there had been a number of people eager to look at the farm. There was the farmer from Aberdeen-shire, and the couple from somewhere near Taynuilt. One day, when Marian was away visiting a friend, her mother told her there had been a youngish man with an English accent, who'd come with Mr Jamieson.

Some days, Marian felt downcast. Suppose someone bought it who was difficult to deal with, who didn't want to keep Geordie and Bob on? Where would they go?

But now, as she looked out of her bedroom window, Marian felt that things would work out. Somehow, she was convinced that something important was about to happen, that everything would be different when they moved. She was still young enough to enjoy a change and realised that she had been in a rut.

A movement caught her eye. It was Davy, the postman, coming up the path.

'Good morning,' she called. 'Fine day.'

'It is that,' he replied cheerfully. 'Nothing much today, Marian, just a brown envelope for your mother.'

The girl smiled. Davy knew everything that was going on.

'I'll be right down,' she said, knowing that he usually enjoyed a cup of tea and a scone before continuing on his round.

She recognised the envelope, and could hardly wait for her mother to open it.

'Open it, Mother,' she urged. 'It's from Mr Jamieson. Oh, I hope it's good news!'

But Betsy wasn't in any hurry.

'Och, it'll just be something else to sign,' she muttered.

'No, I'm sure this one's important. I feel it in my bones.'

Betsy passed over the letter.

'He's found a buyer,' she said softly.

Marian scanned the letter.

'A buyer from England,' she read. 'He wants to take over at Quarter Day. That's not long.'

'Have you seen my homework jotter?' Elspeth slammed the kitchen door behind her.

'I never knew anyone like you for losing things,' her mother reprimanded. 'It'll be where you left it.'

'But I don't know where that is!' Elspeth wailed.

'I'll help you look for it, else you're going to be late.' Marian rose from the table.

Her young sister had been upset about the move at first. But there were so many other things to think about – her music lessons, the school concert, playing in the second hockey eleven. Elspeth's days were full.

'We're moving at Quarter Day,' Marian told her.

'When's that?' Elspeth asked.

'In June. Not long to go.'

'Can I have a bedroom to myself? Can I take my piano?'

Elspeth's piano! They hadn't thought of that.

'I doubt there'll be enough room.' Betsy's brow furrowed. 'We'll have to see...'

'But I need it. I must practise!'

Marian tried to soothe her.

'Maybe the new owner will let you practise here for a bit. Perhaps they won't use the parlour all that much...'

'You'll ask them, won't you?' Elspeth pleaded.

'I promise I'll ask...'

When Elspeth had gone, Betsy turned to her daughter.

'Does he say anything about Geordie and Bob?'

'They'll be kept on.' Marian sounded relieved. 'The new owner's agreed.'

'And Jess? Would he want her, too?' Betsy continued.

'Well, he'd be daft not to,' Marian pointed out. Jess came every spring to help with the cleaning. After all these years, she was more of a friend than an employee.

The next few weeks were hectic and Jess came up to the farm most days.

'I don't know what we'd do without you,' Betsy said. 'How are we going to manage?'

'You'll be fine,' Jess reassured her. 'And Geordie and Bob will still be here, so maybe the new man will need me sometimes, too. Though,' she looked round with satisfaction, 'it's like a new pin here. I don't think there's much heavy work to do.'

'Jess, you've been a good friend. Thank you for all your help…' Betsy's eyes filled.

'You're doing the right thing, you and those two lassies.' The other woman patted her hand. 'You'll not regret it.'

Now, Marian thought, there was hardly a time when she hadn't been washing floors, turning out cupboards and helping her mother to make decisions about what to keep and what to throw out. That was the hardest part.

She found Betsy one day, sitting quietly in what had been William's room.

'Mother?' Marian probed gently. 'Is everything all right? You're miles away.'

Her mother turned.

'I found William's cricket bat.' She smiled. 'Remember how excited he was when he was first chosen to play for the team…?'

Marian was silent. There was nothing she could say that would comfort her mother.

But after a moment or two, Betsy rose.

'Do you think the cricket club would like it? It's a fine bat – maybe some young lad could use it.'

'That's a very good idea.' Marian laid her hand gently on her mother's, needing no other words.

Removal day was frantic, right from the

time the family awoke to the soft grey dawn. Marian looked out of her window, seeing the familiar scene for the last time. Then she shook herself. No time for brooding today, there was work to be done.

Geordie and Bob helped to move much of the heavy furniture with a horse and cart.

'Let me come, please!' Elspeth begged, and she was in seventh heaven, balanced precariously on a kitchen chair on top of the cart.

Jess had scrubbed and polished the cottage and it was all fresh and bright when they arrived. She'd picked a bunch of flowers from the garden and put them in an old stoneware jug.

Betsy looked around with pleasure.

'How nice it all looks!'

Elspeth was beside herself with excitement. She rushed upstairs to the little room she had claimed as her own, and before long was setting out her treasured collection of favourite school stories on the shelf.

The next week was just as busy, settling into the cottage, tending to the garden which had been neglected for some time.

'I saw him.' Elspeth burst into the cottage one day after school. 'I saw the new man.'

'What new man?' Marian was trying to

find space for the china and ornaments that she had unpacked.

'Oh, you!' Elspeth said impatiently. 'The new man at our house – what *was* our house,' she added. 'I saw him driving up the road in a big grey car. It must have been him.'

'Oh, well,' Marian said, 'I expect we'll set eyes on him soon enough.'

She didn't know if she wanted to meet the new owner. He was from England – that much she knew. And maybe he had a wife who didn't want to move to Perthshire. Maybe she was a city type who wouldn't understand the dialect of the local people...

Marian checked herself. This was nonsense. They knew very little about the new owner, except that he'd readily agreed to all the terms. Geordie and Bob would be safe in their jobs and Jess would come in to help from time to time, just as it had always been. But things *were* different now.

'Marian!' Elspeth tried to claim her sister's attention. 'What about my piano? It's still there ... there's got to be room for it here.'

'Of course.' Marian looked round the little sitting-room. 'We'll make space somehow. I'll go up to the house and speak to the new owner.'

'Miss Macfarlane says I've got to keep practising.'

'Don't fret, Elspeth. I'll see about it. It's just that everything's been so busy the past week... But I will. I promise.'

The next week, Marian set off to walk the short distance up the road to the farmhouse. It was a perfect June day and she could see for miles across the fields. She walked slowly, enjoying the peace of the countryside.

When she reached the farmhouse, she paused. It seemed so strange to ring the bell. But she reminded herself it wasn't her home any longer. Tugging at the heavy brass bell, she waited patiently on the doorstep.

There was no reply. Marian looked around. There seemed to be no signs of activity.

Perhaps there wasn't anyone at home. Would it be taking a liberty if she had a quick look round, gathered up any oddments that had been left behind, and measured the piano, to see if it would fit in the cottage?

'Go ahead,' she told herself. 'It's a waste of time coming otherwise.'

So, despite her misgivings, she pushed open the door and went through the familiar hall. There was still no sign of life. She looked into the dining-room but there was no-one there.

What about the piano? It had always been in the little parlour upstairs, the room that had been her father's study. After he died it became a parlour where the family sat in winter.

Marian would sit at the big rolltop desk to do her accounts. And in the corner stood the piano.

The door of the parlour was ajar. She pushed it open, and stopped, stifling a little scream. Her hand at her mouth, she leaned against the doorpost, trembling.

There, in the big chair that had been her father's, was – no, it couldn't be! But that was how he used to sit, leaning back, a book on his knee.

It lasted only a moment, because the figure in the chair whirled round and rose.

'I'm so sorry...' Marian stammered. 'I didn't mean to intrude. Only I thought...'

He was tall, with fair hair and clear blue eyes.

'Did I alarm you?' He seemed rather amused by Marian's dismay. 'I'm sorry.'

'No,' she apologised hastily, 'it was my own fault. I shouldn't have walked right in, but there was no reply when I rang.' She felt flustered and very foolish.

'I'm afraid I was deep in thought,' he said. 'I didn't hear the bell...

'Won't you sit down? You must be Miss Marian Meldrum...?'

She nodded.

'My name is Paul Holt,' he said. 'I'm the new owner, and I'm very pleased to meet you...'

Chapter Two

'Well, this is a surprise. I wasn't expecting visitors.' Paul offered his hand. After a moment's hesitation, Marian took it.

'Won't you sit down?'

She moved, a little reluctantly, to a chair in the corner. How could she have been so foolish? This tall stranger with the clipped voice was nothing like her father. Her mind had played a trick, but she felt a moment's pang of loss for the well-loved figure, his deep, kindly voice and hearty laugh. How she missed him!

'I hope,' she began, struggling to be polite, 'that you've settled in comfortably?'

'Yes, I'm beginning to feel more at home,' he replied pleasantly. 'Of course, there's a lot to be done.' He waved a hand around the room. 'I plan to modernise the entire house in time.'

'I see…' Marian found it hard to keep her voice steady.

'I'm putting in electric light,' he went on. 'It should make a great difference. It's so

45

much more efficient.'

'We've always managed with paraffin lamps,' Marian said evenly.

'Ah, yes. Old fashioned, but, granted, they cast a warm glow.'

Marian hated the note of patronage she detected in his voice.

'And you have other plans?' she asked.

'All in good time.'

He smiled at her, unaware of the way she clasped her hands tightly in her lap and the fact that she was biting her lip to keep it from trembling.

'I'm keeping on the two men – Geordie and Bob,' he continued. 'They're good workers, both of them. But I'll need other help on the farm, especially if I'm going to give over more land to the rasps.'

'I, that is, we ... had planned to hire pickers from Dundee.'

'Yes, I'll look into that.' He nodded. 'There's a lot to be done.'

He hadn't, Marian noticed, mentioned a wife. If he was alone, who was looking after him?

Almost as if he could read her thoughts, he spoke again.

'I've taken on a housekeeper – Bob's wife. Jess has been with your family for some years, I believe?'

'She helped us at harvest time, and with the spring cleaning, and I don't know what we would have done without her. Especially when William…'

'I know,' he sympathised. 'I'm sorry about your brother.'

'Thank you,' Marian said stiffly. She was anxious to keep a distance between herself and this confident stranger. 'Well, I hope you will soon be settled in.'

She rose to go. There was nothing more to be said to this man who was sitting in her father's chair, behaving as if he had every right to be there.

Which he has, a small voice inside Marian's head insisted, but she refused to listen.

'I trust I didn't disturb you too much,' she forced herself to say.

'It doesn't matter,' he replied coolly. 'I didn't mind the interruption. I was merely reading.'

'Then I won't detain you from your book any longer.'

'Was there something you wanted?' he asked.

Suddenly, a door banged shut somewhere at the foot of the stairs. Paul leapt to his feet.

'What was that? That noise!'

Marian, about to go, turned in surprise.

'It's only a door slamming. I must have left the hall door ajar.'

'Oh, just like that!' He spoke sharply. 'I'm surprised at you, Miss Meldrum! Born and brought up on a farm, and you haven't enough sense to close a door or a gate behind you.'

Marian flushed. She glared at him. What an impossible man! No-one had ever spoken to her like this before. What rudeness, and what a fuss to make just because she'd left a door open.

With a great effort of will, she resisted the impulse to snap back at him.

'I do apologise, Mr Holt,' she said icily. 'Good afternoon.'

Somehow, she got herself out of the room and closed the door, quietly but firmly.

Behind her, Paul clenched his fists, staring bleakly out of the window. How could he have given way like that in front of a complete stranger? Not even a sympathetic one, either!

He could not, he thought bitterly, have behaved more foolishly, and in the presence of that prickly, opinionated young woman who obviously resented his even being here.

Suddenly, he found himself shaking. His

reaction to these unexpected noises was extreme. But he couldn't help it. How long would it be before he could forget the sounds of war; the gunfire, the exploding shells?

Gradually, he became calmer and turned to his desk. With a sigh, he picked up some papers in an attempt to focus his mind. One thing was clear, he thought grimly. Miss Meldrum would not come calling again...

Oh, well, if she was inclined to resent his presence, that was no bad thing. He had quite enough to think about.

As Marian ran down the stairs, her heart pounding, Jess came out of the kitchen.

'Miss Marian?' she called. 'It *is* you! I thought I heard a familiar voice. Come away in and have a cup of tea.'

Marian smiled, a little shakily, at the older woman.

'I won't today, Jess, thanks. I've got to get home.' She paused. 'Mr Holt tells me you're going to be his housekeeper?'

'Aye, isn't that grand?' Jess beamed. 'I think I'll be a help to him, settling in. I'm right at home here in the kitchen.'

'He's lucky to have you.' Marian tried to smile. 'I'm glad you're staying.'

'Mind you,' Jess went on, 'I'll miss your

mother. We had some fine blethers.'

'Times change,' Marian said, her voice strained. 'You'll come down and see us, Jess, won't you? My mother would be glad of a visit.'

'I'll be sure to do that, Miss Marian. Now, you're sure you'll not stay?'

The girl shook her head.

'I must get back.'

She hurried down the lane, her head in a whirl. Despite being glad to see Jess again, the short exchange hadn't made her forget her humiliating encounter with Paul Holt.

Perhaps she had shown a little resentment at seeing him so comfortably ensconced in her old home. But surely he had no call to be so rude?

She paused, looking back at the farmhouse. Well, it wasn't *her* home any more. Best to put the past behind her. There was no point in upsetting herself over something she couldn't change.

She hurried on and, by the time she reached the cottage, she was almost her usual calm, unruffled self.

'Hello!' Elspeth was skipping on the front path, but stopped when she saw her sister at the gate. 'Where have you been?'

'I went for a walk. And I've been up to the farm.'

'And did you see the new man?' Elspeth said eagerly. 'Did you see his grand car? And, oh, Marian, did you ask him about my piano?'

'Yes,' Marian murmured. 'I saw him.'

'Well, what did he say?'

Elspeth flung down her skipping rope and clung on to her sister's arm.

'Can my piano be moved down here, or maybe I could go up there and practise? What did he say?'

'I didn't ask him.'

'You didn't ask him?' Elspeth's voice rose. 'But you know I need to keep practising, and you *promised*–'

Marian's temper flared.

'Don't you ever think of anyone but yourself?' She rounded on her young sister. 'What a selfish little madam you are sometimes, Elspeth Meldrum!'

The young girl stared at Marian as if she couldn't believe her ears. Then she turned and, bursting into tears, rushed into the cottage.

'What on earth's the matter?' The girls' mother appeared in the doorway. 'What's wrong with Elspeth?'

'Oh, don't ask me. I seem to be upsetting everyone today.' Marian's voice trembled.

She followed Elspeth upstairs without another word, leaving Betsy looking on in complete bewilderment.

During the long sunny days that followed, Marian did her best to avoid the road to the farm.

Normally, it was her favourite time of the year. She enjoyed seeing the dog roses and campion in the hedgerows, and loved the freshness of the early mornings, when she was often up and about before anyone else.

But, this year, there seemed no point in getting up early. There was nothing to do at the cottage. Her mother worked happily in the small kitchen, baking and ironing, or contentedly polishing the worn but treasured pieces of brass they'd brought from the farm.

As for Elspeth – she was outdoors nearly all the time with her friends, revelling in the long summer days, eagerly waiting for the school holidays.

There was no reason, Marian told herself sternly, why she should feel so out of sorts. The family had settled comfortably into the cottage. For the first time in years she didn't have to rise at dawn and see to the hundred and one chores about the farm. She was free to do what ever she liked whenever she liked!

But something was missing.

Marian shook herself. This self-pity simply wouldn't do. There was still work to be done – shopping, for one thing. She picked up the basket and the shopping list.

'Is there anything you need, Mother?'

'Yes, dear. Some more of this lace edging, if you'd call into Greive's on your way.' Betsy spread out the white cotton blouse she was finishing for Elspeth.

How contented her mother was, Marian thought. Such a change of circumstances and yet she never complained. Marian felt suddenly ashamed of herself.

'That blouse is going to be really smart. Elspeth will be pleased.'

'Away you go,' her mother said lightly. 'It's a grand day for a walk into Blair.'

Marian had finished her errands and was walking down the High Street when she heard someone calling her name.

She turned to look at the young doctor who was hurrying down the street towards her.

'You look busy, Robert.' She smiled.

'I've just come from a call and I'm on my

way to another. I haven't seen you for a while. How are you all settling in at the cottage?'

'Oh, we're doing away fine. It's quite a change, though.'

'I'm sure it is.' His dark eyes were sympathetic. 'You must have found leaving the farmhouse a wrench.'

'Well, in a way. But we were glad to move when it came to it.'

What a good friend Robert was, Marian thought. She remembered him as a youngster. He was always protective and kindly towards other children at school – the ones who were a bit left out of things. It was typical of Robert that he understood her feelings, though she'd tried to make light of them.

'And your mother, and Elspeth?'

'Oh, they're as happy as the day is long! Elspeth has plenty to do, and Mother seems contented. It's all turned out very well.'

'And you?'

'I'm fine, as always,' Marian answered, but something in her tone made Robert look at her sharply.

This wasn't the Marian he remembered; the lively girl, full of energy. She was far too pale and her eyes appeared dull and strained.

'Look,' he said, 'I can't stop now. I've another call to make. But would your

54

mother mind if I dropped in one day, just to say hello?'

'She'd be pleased to see you – we all would.'

'Right, then. I'll do that.'

Marian turned to go, but he stayed a moment, watching her as she walked slowly down the street. Something was wrong. Every instinct told him so.

A week later, Robert found himself not far from the Meldrums' cottage. He had no further calls and was on his way home, enjoying the drive through the countryside.

On an impulse, he decided to call on them.

'Anyone at home?'

He rapped the brass knocker. Almost immediately, Betsy appeared, wiping her hands on her apron.

'Robert! It's been such a long time since we saw you. Come away in! What have you been doing with yourself? Well now, that's a daft question, isn't it? I know fine how busy you are, and what a grand help you must be to your father in the practice.

'And he's well? And your mother?'

Talking all the time, she led the young man into the kitchen.

'You'll not object to a seat at the kitchen table?'

He laughed, looking around him appreciatively.

'You've certainly made it all very comfortable and homely, Mrs Meldrum.'

'Oh, we're settling in fine.' Betsy busied herself filling the kettle. 'I'm fair enjoying living in the cottage.

'But I'm a wee bit worried about Marian,' she continued. 'She's not herself at all – a bit snappy, ready to take offence. She's not interested in things the way she used to be.'

'Where is she?'

'Working in the garden. It's a bit overgrown.'

'Then I'll wait for that cup of tea if you don't mind,' Robert said, already on his feet. 'I'll go and have a word with her.'

'I wish you would.' Betsy smiled. 'Maybe you can talk some sense into her!'

At the far end of the garden, Marian was hacking at a patch of brambles, a look of determination on her face.

'My, that looks like hard work!' Robert said as he approached her.

She stopped, wiping a hand across her brow.

'Hello, Robert. What brings you to our

56

door today?'

'I've finished my rounds so I thought I'd call in for a cup of tea. See how you're all settling in.'

'It's good to see you.'

'Can I help? You've quite a job on your hands there.'

'Oh, it doesn't matter.' Marian sighed, running a hand over her hair. 'There's no hurry. I was clearing this patch for something to do, really.'

'That's what's wrong, isn't it?' Robert said gently.

'Wrong?'

'Yes. Come on, Marian, we're old friends. You don't need to pretend with me. You're bored. That's the trouble, isn't it?'

'I suppose it is.' Marian made a face. 'There's no farm work to be done, no accounts... I'm not the type to sit around doing nothing, Robert. I've thought of trying to get a teaching post.'

'Yes, I remember you trained as a teacher.' Marian sighed.

'At the beginning of the war. But then I had to give it up – I was needed on the farm.' She said it in a matter-of-fact way, without a trace of self-pity.

'So you're thinking about going back to it?'

Marian shrugged her shoulders.

'I'd like to, but … I don't know. It's years since I taught. I'd be out of practice. Those men coming back from the war; they'll need the work. It was different when they were all away. Who would give *me* a job?'

'Well, perhaps I can help you there. My father was talking to Mr Lindsay the other day. You know, the headmaster at the village school? One of his staff has had to retire early, so he's looking for a replacement.'

Marian looked thoughtful.

'I suppose I could go and see him…'

Robert nodded.

'I don't see why not. Of course, the decision would be the school board's, but if he thought you should apply, it would be a good recommendation.'

'It's worth a try.' Marian straightened up. 'He can only turn me down. And if he does, I'll try elsewhere.'

'That's the spirit!' Robert was delighted to see Marian regain some of her old sparkle.

'Come on,' she said. 'I'm pretty sure Mother will have the kettle on. You've time for a cup?'

Next day, Marian arranged to see the headmaster.

She dressed in her best grey Sunday suit, with a white pleated voile blouse and, as an afterthought, pinned a dark red rose to her jacket.

It was only another week until the school broke up for the summer holidays, but the children were still at their desks, heads down, struggling over long division.

Marian's heart went out to them. Surely, on such a fine summer's day, they might have had an extra playtime, out in the sunshine? But she knew that wasn't Mr Lindsay's way. He was fair, but strict.

She took a deep breath and went in to meet the headmaster.

'So you're William Meldrum's sister?' he greeted her. 'I taught him. A wild laddie, he was.'

Marian was pleased that he didn't offer formal words of sympathy, but remembered her brother as an unruly schoolboy. She liked the headmaster's steady gaze and direct way of speaking.

She decided honesty was the best policy.

'I've had very little experience, Mr Lindsay – mainly teaching practice. And I gave it up to take on the farm, when William...' She laid her certificates on the table. 'The minister, Mr Ross, has given me a reference.'

'You seem very determined to take up the post, Miss Meldrum,' he said wryly.

'I think I'd make a good job of it.' Marian lifted her chin.

'We'll see.' Mr Lindsay was non-committal. He asked a number of questions and Marian answered as calmly and confidently as she could.

At last, he rose and shook her hand.

'I'll need to put it to the board, Miss Meldrum, but I think I can safely say they'll accept my recommendation. They'll want to interview you, of course, but I would hope, all being in order, you could join us for the autumn term.'

Just then the janitor rang the bell for playtime, and there was a sudden rush towards the door as the children burst out into the sunshine.

Marian found herself smiling at the children as she walked down the playground and out of the gate. Her spirits rose.

She realised this opportunity was what she had been waiting for ... to teach here, to be doing something she loved, to be *useful* again.

'There's dozens of them! I saw them coming off the buses!'

An old woman, pausing with her shopping basket outside the butcher's in Allan Street, shook her head.

'They're mostly from Dundee,' her friend supplied. 'Poor souls, it'll be a grand treat for them being in the fine fresh air at the berries, away from all that dirt and smoke for a few months.'

'Likely they'll be wild, the bairns – cooped up all the winter,' her friend said gloomily.

'Well, they'll be staying in the huts...' the other woman said more optimistically. 'The Tin City. There's a shop and all for them. And they're decent folk, I'm sure, trying to bring up their bairns the best they can. They can't help being poor, after all.'

'Aye...' Her friend was still doubtful. 'But they're still strangers, not used to country ways.'

Paul Holt wondered, too, how he would cope with the influx from the city when he saw the berry pickers making their way along the road. So many children!

There was a fine crop of berries this summer; he'd never have managed to harvest it without help. But seasonal workers meant more responsibility, too...

Geordie had been guarded when Paul asked him to supervise.

'I'll do my best, sir,' he'd said. 'But you'll understand we're busy enough on the farm...'

'I'll go down to the fields myself, as often as I can,' Paul had promised. 'I'm sure the parents will try to keep the children under control.'

He regretted his words almost immediately, when Jess appeared in the kitchen, dragging behind her a boy about nine or ten years old. His hair stood up on end, his face was smeared with dirt, and he wore an old shirt, several sizes too big for him, and ragged trousers.

'I found him in the yard, chasing the hens! He's one of the pickers.'

She gave the boy a shake, and he looked back at her boldly, apparently unperturbed.

'What's your name?' Paul gave a sigh. This wasn't a good start.

'Dougie.'

'Sir,' Jess prompted.

He took no notice.

'Dougie – what?'

'Dougie Mackay.'

Paul had little or no experience of children. His friends' offspring were well-mannered, tidy and practically invisible! He'd seldom met this kind of child, especially one who

62

gazed insolently back at him.

'Why were you chasing the hens?'

'I wanted a feather – for an Indian head-dress,' the boy explained as if it was all very logical.

'I see.' Paul was at a loss. 'Shouldn't you be with your family?

'Come on,' he said with a sigh after meeting with a resolutely silent stare. 'I'll take him back to the fields with me, Jess.'

As they walked down to the fields, the boy trudging sullenly beside Paul, they passed Marian on her way to the village shop. She greeted Paul coolly, glancing with some curiosity at the boy.

One of the pickers, she thought. And it looked as though he was in trouble already with Mr Holt...

She shrugged. It was nothing to do with her.

Paul spoke briefly to some of the families who were already at work in the fields. Some answered him, while others just nodded and turned away.

'They canna understand him,' Geordie said to Bob, as they watched Paul walk up the rows of rasps. 'It's the English accent. He might as well be talking double Dutch!'

'Has he been misbehavin'?' Dougie's

mother accosted Paul.

He looked blankly at her as a torrent of words poured out.

'She's saying you're not to put up with any nonsense,' Geordie translated. 'Dougie's always up to something. You're to let her know if he's any trouble.'

'Yes ... well...' Paul felt inadequate. How was he going to cope with these people when they couldn't even understand each other?

As the days went by, he became even more anxious. There was a great deal to do on the farm: accounts to be gone through, agricultural representatives to see, catalogues of new machinery to read, market day in Blair.

He knew Geordie and Bob were reluctant to leave their everyday work to supervise the pickers. But who else would do it?

Paul wished that he'd been able to make friends with Marian. She'd been born and brought up here, and could have talked to the pickers and easily sorted out any problems. There had been some murmuring the other day, some grievance about the length of the dinner break.

He hoped Geordie had been able to settle it. The last thing he wanted was a mutiny!

Suddenly, Paul felt very isolated. If only he

had someone to talk to, seek advice from…

And there was the rift with his parents. He tried to look on the bright side, to sound cheerful and positive when he wrote to Sarah. But sometimes, when he tossed and turned at night, he couldn't help wondering if he'd made the right decision in coming to Scotland.

Sarah's letter in reply was brisk and down to earth. Paul read it over the breakfast table.

You ask about our parents. Well, of course Father is disappointed. Rather more than that, really. I'm sorry to tell you, but he has refused to have you in the house again. And now, he won't even mention your name. I'm sorry to send such depressing news, but you probably realised that he would react in this way.

I've tried – and so has Mother – to put your point of view. But he won't listen. I'd say, don't write, or try to explain. It will only make things worse. Mother is torn between the two of you…

Paul laid down his spoon. He had no appetite now. Had he been selfish? Wouldn't it have been better to at least have given the factory a try?

He picked up the letter and continued reading.

Now all this sounds gloomy. But you mustn't

give up. You have done the right thing, Paul. I expect it'll be hard at first. Maybe they're a bit suspicious of you and your accent.

I wish I were a bit nearer, and we could talk things over. But why don't you take on a manager – someone who could see to the day-to-day things for you? Someone whom you trust, who's good with people. It would save you a lot of trouble and you wouldn't feel so alone!

You don't say much about the former owner – except that one rather difficult meeting. Pity. She might have been a help. She sounds as if she'll keep her distance.

You don't say anything either about the girls you've met – don't you have time for a social life, up there?

Paul laid down the letter. He re-read it later, but as he went about the farm, he kept thinking of Sarah's idea. Someone he could trust … someone who was used to dealing with people. Someone whose was cheerful, not afraid of hard work.

And then it all seemed perfectly clear. Sergeant Fordyce. He'd been in Paul's regiment, and Paul remembered him as a solid, reliable man who coped calmly with all the horrors of trench warfare. More than once, Paul had been grateful for his quick reactions and sturdy commonsense.

Paul had often wondered how the sergeant was coping with civilian life – he hoped he'd found work in a post where he'd be valued.

He reproached himself for not getting in touch with the sergeant sooner, to see how he was getting on.

Sergeant Fordyce was townbred, but he could manage people – that had been proved time and again. He might be the very person for the farm manager's job!

There was no harm in writing anyway, Paul decided. He picked up the pen, feeling much more cheerful and optimistic.

Marian, too, felt much happier. In the last week, she'd been interviewed by the school board and had been offered a post, starting at the end of August when the school re-opened.

She seldom walked past the berryfields, but she'd seen – she couldn't help seeing – the groups of pickers who made their way daily from the tin huts where they were lodged.

One day, walking homeward, she rounded the corner of the road and found a woman not much older than herself with a toddler and a young boy. The woman was leaning against the trunk of a tree, her hand to her side, while the children stood, watching her.

'Are you all right?' Marian hurried forward.

'I'm fine.' The woman looked up. 'I just took a stitch in my side. It's nothing.'

'I'll walk along the road with you,' Marian suggested, noticing the woman's tired face. 'Can I carry your bag?'

To begin with the woman was silent, but when she recovered her breath, she looked around her approvingly.

'My, but this is grand!' She sighed contentedly.

'You're from Dundee?' Marian asked.

'Aye, and it's as good as a holiday for the bairns,' the woman responded cheerfully. She broke off to call over to her older child. 'Dougie! Stop that! You'll ruin your boots!'

'Are you enjoying your holiday, Dougie?' Marian asked, having a special liking for tough, small boys.

''S better than school,' Dougie replied dourly.

'He doesna' like school,' his mother confided. 'He's never out of trouble. They canna do anything wi' him – he canna even read yet.'

'Is that right, Dougie?' Marian asked.

'Aye!' The boy sounded quite proud of

68

the fact.

They walked on for a bit and Marian left them at the turning towards the cottage.

She turned back to watch them trudging along the road – the woman, now carrying the toddler, and Dougie weaving from side to side of the road, kicking a stone.

They don't have much, she thought. Life was obviously hard for the family. She'd taken an instant liking to the dumpy, rosy-cheeked mother and her uncomplaining cheerfulness. And Dougie was just the sort of child she liked, full of character and spirit.

She would have liked to have been able to help them…

'I'll just clear the things away and set the table for the morning, then I'll be off.'

'Thank you, Jess.' Paul looked up from his desk. 'That was a grand dinner.'

'Rabbit pie's tasty.' Jess beamed at him. She moved to draw the curtains. 'My, it's a wild night, right enough.'

'Do you often get storms like this in August?' Paul asked casually.

'Sometimes. It's been close and heavy the past few days – you could tell there was thunder on the way. Ah, well, it'll clear the air.'

She closed the door quietly behind her, and Paul turned again to the letters on his desk. Nothing from his father – well, that was only to be expected. Perhaps in the next few days there would be a reply from the sergeant. Paul's letter should have reached him by now.

He smiled as he picked up another letter. Now this was one he would need to answer, and promptly. It was in a round, childish hand.

Dear Mr Holt,

My name is Elspeth Meldrum and I am learning to play the piano...

He read on. Of course, the child had to practise and, clearly, she was enthusiastic. Perhaps she could come here when he was out during the day...

He gave a little grimace. He had no wish to be deafened with the sound of scales. Nor did he owe any favours to *that* family!

He'd prefer not to meet the elder sister again, he decided, remembering their meeting. But the child – well, perhaps something could be arranged.

There was a violent clap of thunder. It seemed almost overhead. He rose from his desk and drew the curtains aside, looking down on the rain-soaked garden.

It was then he heard the doorbell jangling. He gave a start of surprise. Who on earth would come out on such a night?

As he made his way down the stairs, Jess came out of the kitchen, wiping her hands on her apron.

'Whoever's that?' she said, echoing his thoughts. 'Out on a night like this?'

Paul hurriedly unlatched the big oak door, and as he did so a gust of wind swept through the hall. There was a sudden flash of lightning, and as it forked across the sky, they could see the figure on the doorstep.

'What on earth...' Jess's voice died away as she stared at the woman who clutched the doorpost – a figure in a shabby black coat, soaked to the skin. Paul caught a glimpse of dark eyes in a chalk-white face.

'Come in!' He stretched out a hand towards the woman, who was trembling violently – whether with fear or cold, he couldn't be sure. Together, he and Jess led her into the sitting-room where a fire burned in the grate, and she sank into a chair.

For a moment, Paul and Jess stood looking at her, then Paul took charge.

'Can you make her a hot drink, and maybe find some warm clothes or blankets?'

'I'll do that.' Jess hurried off.

'I think she's ill. We'd better call Doctor Robert.'

Paul stirred the fire into a blaze with the poker, and the girl gave a faint moan as she felt the warmth.

'Who are you? What do you want?' Paul asked gently.

But the girl simply turned her head from side to side, and gave no sign of hearing him.

Outside, the wind howled and the stem of a climbing rose tapped against the window. Who could she be? Where had she come from on such a night?

A few minutes later, Jess appeared again with an armful of blankets.

'I've sent Geordie for the doctor.' She knelt down beside the trembling girl.

'Poor thing!' she said. 'She's soaked through.'

Gently, she drew off the girl's shoes, noticing how flimsy they were and how unsuitable for country roads. She lifted the girl in her arms and took off the shabby black coat.

'Will I make up the spare room bed, Mr Holt? She'll not be fit to go much further on a night like this.'

'Yes, if you would, Jess.' Paul looked up.

Thank goodness his housekeeper was such a sensible, level-headed woman.

Suddenly, in the warmth of the fire, the girl stirred. She moved her head from side to side, and dark eyes met Paul's.

She tried to speak...

'See and keep quiet now,' Jess told her. 'Don't try to talk.'

The girl whispered and Paul craned to hear what she said.

'Merci.' Her eyes closed again.

Paul turned to look at Jess.

'She said *"Merci"*. Thank you...'

'The bed's been kept aired, and I'll put in a hot-water bottle.'

'There's a mystery here,' Paul said firmly. 'But we'll find out more tomorrow. For the moment, the poor girl must be allowed to rest.'

Who is she? Paul wondered at the strange turn the evening had taken. What did she want? And how had she found her way to the farm...?

Chapter Three

'So who is she? Where has she come from?'
Jess looked up at Paul.

He shook his head slowly. 'I've no idea.'

The girl lay back in an armchair. How white and exhausted she looked, Jess thought. She didn't move a muscle as the older woman anxiously watched the clock, waiting for the doctor.

'There's the doorbell. That'll be him now.' Jess moved quickly to answer the door.

'She's in here, Doctor.' She explained quickly what had happened.

Robert didn't waste words. He examined the girl swiftly and capably, then put his stethoscope back in its case. He stood silently for a moment, looking down at her, a slight frown on his face.

'Is she bad, then, Doctor?' Jess asked anxiously.

'No, no,' the young man reassured her. 'There's nothing really wrong. She just needs to rest. She's exhausted. Can you keep her overnight, and I'll come back tomorrow?'

'Of course!' Jess spoke more indignantly than she meant. 'We'd not be turning the poor lass out on a night like this!'

They could hear the gale whistling around the house, and the loose stem of a climbing rose tapping against the window.

Paul had said very little so far. Now, he turned to his housekeeper.

'Is the spare room bed made up, Jess? And do you think you could see the young lady is comfortable?'

'I'll do that,' Jess said briskly. 'There's a pig in the bed...'

'A pig?' Paul looked astonished.

Robert smiled.

'It's a Scots word for a stone hot-water bottle,' he explained. 'Nothing like it for heating the bed.

'Don't try to talk now.' Gently, he helped the girl to her feet. 'That can wait.'

'I'll see her to bed, and bring her a glass of warm milk,' Jess said. 'Come away, now, lass, you'll soon be tucked up fine and warm...'

As the door closed behind them, Paul waved the doctor to a chair.

'Take a seat, Doctor, if you've a moment to spare.'

'I can hang back for a bit. They'll ring me

here if there's another call.'

Robert sat down in one of the big leather armchairs, stretching out his long legs towards the fire.

'You'll be wondering what all this is about,' Paul began hesitantly. 'It's a bit of a mystery.'

'You've no idea who she is?' the doctor asked.

'None whatsoever,' Paul answered. 'I opened the door to find the poor creature looking half drowned. Luckily, Jess is a sensible soul who doesn't panic easily.'

'Yes, she's useful in a crisis, salt of the earth,' Robert agreed. 'What puzzles me is why did the girl come here…?'

'I can't imagine,' Paul mused. 'The farm's out of the way. She must have struggled up the lane.'

'Do you mind if I smoke my pipe?' The doctor felt in his pocket. 'It helps me to think.'

'Go ahead.' Paul lifted another log from the basket and put it on the fire.

'She could have gone into Blair and found lodgings,' Robert said. 'I wonder if she came by train from Dundee?'

'I'd say that she was looking for work,' Paul put in. 'But why turn up at this time of night?'

Robert shook his head.

'I don't think she's used to farm work. Her hands are in too good condition. I'd guess she's a seamstress, or maybe a shop girl...'

He puffed at his pipe thoughtfully.

'There is one clue.' Paul leaned forward. 'After we had helped her in, she looked up and said, *merci.*'

'French?' Robert's eyebrows rose. 'But what on earth would a Frenchwoman be doing here?'

'What indeed?'

'Well, it certainly is a mystery.'

Robert rose to his feet. 'I'll need to be getting back.' He looked at Paul. 'You seem a bit low yourself. Are you feeling all right?'

'I'm fine,' Paul reassured him. 'Just busy, you know. There's a lot to do at this time of year, and I'm still finding my feet.'

Robert nodded sympathetically.

'A farm's hard work, as you're no doubt finding out! Just don't overdo things. And don't worry about that young woman. You and Jess have done all you could. Leave the questions till she's up to it. Tomorrow ... or maybe even the next day.

'Let her rest and she should soon be a lot better. There's nothing wrong with her that a good long sleep won't cure.'

'I can't thank you enough,' Paul said.

'All part of the day's work,' Robert put in cheerfully. 'Don't get up, Mr Holt. I'll see myself out.'

But Paul went with Robert to the door and watched as the lights of the doctor's car disappeared down the lane. Then he turned and closed the big oak door firmly, shutting out the storm.

He went into the kitchen where Jess was hanging the girl's coat and skirt over the clothes-horse in front of the range.

'Is everything all right?' he asked.

'She fell asleep as soon as her head touched the pillow, poor lass.'

Jess glanced at Paul. How tired he looked!

'Don't you fret,' she said in her kindly, matter-of-fact way. 'I'll sleep here tonight, and I can see to her if she's wakeful.'

'Thank you.' Paul smiled. 'I'm really grateful.'

'Och, it's nothing,' Jess said briskly, and he thought again how fortunate he was to have 'inherited' her from the Meldrums.

Once he had gone back to the study, Jess turned again to the clothes-horse. She pursed her lips thoughtfully as she hung the rest of the girl's clothing to dry out.

Everything was well made, though the

material itself was shabby.

The collar and buttonholes were clean but worn and the tucks on the simple white blouse had been done by hand.

It appeared the girl came from a humble background. And if she had made her clothes herself, she was a clever seamstress. Her shoes – Jess tut-tutted as she stuffed newspaper inside them, and put them to dry out – were thin, fashionable; not meant for walking the countryside.

The little black case she had carried in with her could shed no light on the mystery. It was locked.

'You're getting too inquisitive,' Jess chided herself. 'Just take good care of the poor lass, whoever she is, and see she doesn't catch cold from that soaking. We'll find out soon enough where she's come from.'

But, all the same, as she filled the kettle for a last cup of tea, she couldn't help wondering. Who was this girl?

'What a dreadful night!' Marian opened the kitchen window and looked out.

'It's still raining,' she observed. 'It'll be too wet to work at the berries today.'

And then she remembered, with a little pang, that it wasn't her concern any more.

She told herself she should be thankful for not having to worry about the weather...

She started to lay the table for breakfast, while Betsy, already looking wide awake and trim in a fresh print apron, was stirring the porridge.

'Did you sleep through the storm, Mother?'

Betsy nodded.

'I never heard a thing.'

'It kept me awake half the night!'

Marian took down the cups and saucers from the dresser.

'Where's Elspeth?'

'She's still in bed. I'll give her another call in a minute,' Betsy said comfortably.

Marian poured out the tea, enjoying the luxury of having time to spare. Soon, she'd be starting teaching at the school, and in the meantime, she'd begun to help young Dougie Mackay learn to read. She'd found the boy was a quick learner.

Elspeth was yawning over her porridge, when there was a loud knock at the door.

'Will you see who that is, Marian?' Betsy glanced at the clock. 'It's early for visitors.'

Marian opened the door, half expecting the postman. Instead, there stood Mrs Mackay, holding her younger child firmly by the hand with Dougie behind her.

'Mrs Mackay!' Marian was startled. 'This is a surprise. Are you not at the berries today?'

'It's too wet to work the day.'

'Won't you come in?' Marian invited, as the woman hesitated.

'Thank you kindly,' she said with some dignity. 'Mind and wipe your feet,' she told Dougie sharply. 'And don't touch anything.'

Dougie gave Marian the now-familiar lopsided grin and followed his mother inside.

Mrs Mackay hesitated at the kitchen door.

'Go on in,' Marian urged her. 'Mother, this is Mrs Mackay, and Dougie, and … I don't know the name of the little one.'

'She's called Lizzie.'

Mrs Mackay had a tight grip on the child's hand – and she glared at Dougie, who was gazing at the remains of breakfast on the table.

'You'll sit down, Mrs Mackay, and have a cup of tea?' Betsy said warmly, drawing out a chair. 'Elspeth, will you put the kettle on?'

The girl sniffed. In her opinion the berry pickers were a bit rough, and here was Mother inviting them into the kitchen and offering them tea! And Marian, behaving as

81

if they were friends...

Elspeth rose with an ill grace to put the kettle on.

'I've to tidy my room,' she said loftily before going upstairs.

'I hope you aren't too uncomfortable in the tents in all this rain,' Betsy began. 'You must be soaked through, sometimes.'

'Oh, we manage all right,' Mrs Mackay said placidly.

'Here,' Betsy offered, 'let me take Lizzie on my knee. My you're a big girl, aren't you? How old is she, Mrs Mackay?'

'Gone three.'

'A fine wee girl.' Betsy smiled, undoing the child's bonnet. 'There you are.'

Mrs Mackay delved into the large basket she carried and pulled out her purse.

'I've come to pay for Dougie's lessons,' she said firmly. 'It's good of you, Miss, teaching him to read, and he's getting on fine – aren't you, Dougie?'

'Aye,' Dougie replied absently, his eyes on the table.

'I wouldn't dream of taking payment,' Marian said staunchly. 'I enjoy teaching Dougie, and he's doing very well.' She smiled at the boy, who looked a little abashed.

'I like to pay my way, Miss.' Mrs Mackay

counted out some coins. 'I don't like to be in debt.'

'There's no question of paying,' Marian told her firmly.

'Are you sure?' Mrs Mackay paused.

'I'm glad to do it. It keeps my hand in.'

'Good! That's settled.' Betsy rose to pour the tea. 'Dougie, could you take a piece of bread and jam?'

The boy's face brightened and he wolfed down the food.

'He's always hungry,' Mrs Mackay said apologetically.

'Just a growing boy. Now,' Betsy began, sitting down at the table. 'Tell us how you're getting on. Is it your first time at the berries? And how are you managing with this wee one?'

Mrs Mackay cupped both hands around her steaming cup. She looked tired, Betsy thought. The children would be a handful. Was there a Mr Mackay, she wondered?

As if she could read Betsy's thoughts, Mrs Mackay spoke between sips of tea.

'We've been coming two or three years. We do it to get away from the town – it's grand in the fresh air. And we're well looked after. The Temperance ladies that run the canteen at Essendy – they're really kind.

'The canteen's open early, half-past six in the morning. You can get your breakfast – porridge and kippers and eggs and a lot more – and then your dinner – soup and meat and pudding ... we're really lucky.' She sighed.

'I wish my man could be here, too. It would do him good.'

'Has he been ill?' Betsy was sympathetic.

'It's his lungs,' Mrs Mackay explained. 'The doctor said it was with the kind of work he did in the mill all these years. He tried to join up, but they wouldn't take him.

'And now,' she leaned forward, encouraged by Betsy's kindly understanding, 'I don't know what to do with him. He says there's better men than him were killed while he was at home, safe. He goes over it, again and again. But he wasn't fit to go.'

'Then he shouldn't feel like that,' Betsy said firmly. 'And is he no better?'

'He's got another job now, at an office down by the docks. We need the money,' she explained. 'That's why I bring the bairns to the berries. Dougie's a good picker, when he's no' bein' a wee menace! We get three farthings a pound for the first three pickings and a penny a pound after that. It soon adds up.

'And the bairns grow that fast – the money we get at the berries buys their shoes and clothes.'

Betsy felt a rush of admiration for this stalwart little woman, who stated her position so simply and without self-pity, and was so fiercely independent.

'Ah, well, that's life.' Mrs Mackay smiled. 'We'd best be off now. Thank you kindly for the tea.'

'Wait a minute, dear.'

Betsy was suddenly struck by the thought that there were some clothes she no longer needed. But she hesitated. Would it seem as if she was offering charity? Mrs Mackay was proud and Betsy would hate to cause her any embarrassment.

'I might have some things you could use,' she said cautiously. 'They're good, just outgrown. If you could find a use for them, that is?'

'I'd be glad of them,' the woman said simply.

'Then I'll be pleased to look them out for you. If you could drop in maybe in a day or two, I'll have them ready... Oh, Dougie, wait a minute. I think I have something for you, too.'

Betsy went upstairs and into her bedroom.

There was a trunk there, full of things that had belonged to William as a boy.

'Dougie,' she said, when she returned to the kitchen, 'would you like this?' She held out the football. 'I thought you might perhaps...' She paused. 'It was my son's. William was very keen on the game. We ... we lost him in the war. Still, it's good to know another boy will have the use of it.'

Dougie's eyes shone.

'Oh, right, missus,' he said.

'Say thank you,' his mother prompted.

'No need,' Betsy said. The boy's glowing face said it all.

Marian turned aside as the tears pricked her eyes. But when Mrs Mackay and her family left, she could see that her mother was smiling.

'Well, that was quite a night!'

Earlier that morning, Paul Holt had been out in the fields. There would be no picking that day, for it was still raining heavily.

He greeted Jess as cheerfully as he could when he went into the kitchen.

'It's a pity the rain didn't come earlier in the season, for the rasps.'

She nodded.

'The postie's just been – he was telling me

the Ericht was in spate. I've never seen such a storm at this time of year...'

Paul sighed. They were in the middle of the season and, by all accounts, the rasp crop was much lighter than last year. After the gales back in June, so many canes had broken and a lot of damage had been done.

Now, after the rain, maybe there would be a spell of sunshine. But there was another problem, and an immediate one.

'How is she?' he asked.

'She slept like a bairn.' Jess smiled. 'I've taken her a cup of tea, and she'll be down for breakfast.'

'None the worse for her drenching?'

'She'll be all right. Just needs looking after and feeding, poor lass.'

'You'll take some breakfast now?' she asked Paul. 'The porridge is just about ready, and there's a letter for you, on the dresser there.'

'Thanks, Jess.'

Paul picked up the envelope and looked at the carefully formed, unfamiliar handwriting. He turned it over, puzzled. A Glasgow postmark.

He slit open the envelope and pulled out the two pages of notepaper.

Dear Sir ... he read. Of course! It was the

letter he had been waiting for, from Sergeant Fordyce. Paul's spirits rose.

I was glad to hear from you, the sergeant continued. *And hope that you are doing well...*

Paul skimmed the page, shaking his head sadly. Things hadn't been good for Sergeant Fordyce, though he wrote simply and uncomplaining.

I have not been in work this past year. Paul read hastily to the end. *I thank you for your offer, sir. But I am sorry that I cannot accept. I hope you will understand. It is not that I am ungrateful. I remain, yours respectfully...*

Paul laid down the letter, deeply puzzled. Reading between the lines, something was quite plainly wrong. He remembered the sergeant as a cheerful, stoical character who could cope with all kinds of situations. Surely, if he was out of work, he would welcome the offer of a job?

Instead of the letter of acceptance he had expected, though, this was quite definitely a refusal. He looked at the address.

Perhaps he should go and see him face to face, find out what was wrong...

Jess noticed that Paul looked troubled. Then there was a sound and they both looked up. There at the kitchen door stood the girl, hesitating as if she was unsure of her welcome.

She wore a jumper and skirt that belonged to Jess. The clothes hung loose on her thin frame, but still she managed to look somehow elegant. Her dark hair was pinned up on her head, and she held a small black case.

'There you are!' Jess greeted the girl kindly. 'Come away in and sit down.'

Paul stood up, smiling at the girl, who stood, still uncertain, in the doorway.

'How are you this morning?' he asked.

'I am better, thank you.' The girl spoke in halting English.

'Sit down, dear, and have a cup of tea,' Jess told her. 'There's porridge and cream.'

Paul pulled out a chair for the girl, and she sat down, still clutching the little case.

She drank the tea thirstily, and he noticed that the hand that held the cup was trembling.

'There, that'll do you a power of good.'

Jess placed the plate of porridge in front of the girl.

Still hesitating, she picked up the spoon and tasted the porridge. She ate slowly, but finished the bowl, carefully scraping the last drop.

'Thank you,' she said, as Jess poured her

another cup of tea.

As she ate and drank, Paul read through the sergeant's letter again, but from time to time he glanced at the girl.

When he was sure she had finished, he leaned across the table.

'Can you tell us where you have come from? And who you are?'

She looked at him as if she didn't understand.

He repeated the questions.

She shook her head, as if she didn't want to answer.

'What are you looking for? Why have you come here?' Paul continued. 'Last night, you spoke in French...' He paused.

Again, that silence.

'Are you ill? Can we help you? Perhaps you've come looking for work?' he suggested very gently.

Suddenly, the girl's eyes filled with tears, and her hand went to her mouth.

Paul wished Robert was here. As a doctor, he would be used to dealing with people in distress. The last thing Paul wanted to do was to upset the girl more.

'We'll help you if we can,' Paul repeated. 'Now, please, won't you tell us your name?'

'My name is Simone,' she said at last.

Paul smiled at her.

'Well, Simone, won't you tell us what we can do for you, and why you've come here?'

The girl turned to Jess.

'Please, you are Mrs Meldrum, I think?'

'Me?' Jess was startled for a moment, and then she smiled.

'No, dear, I'm the housekeeper. My name's Jess.'

'Mrs Meldrum?' the girl repeated. 'She is not here?'

'They've moved,' Jess explained. 'This is Mr Holt, who's bought the farm from them. They don't live here any longer. They're down in the cottage, not far away.'

The girl rose hastily.

'You have been very kind. Thank you. But I must speak with Mrs Meldrum. I will go and see her.'

'Wait a minute!' Paul began. 'The doctor said you were to rest. You shouldn't go wandering about...'

He looked at Jess, who saw that he was at a bit of a loss.

'Shall I go down there right away and ask Mrs Meldrum and Miss Marian to come up here?' Jess suggested.

'Thank you, Jess.' Paul sighed with relief.

'I won't be long.' Jess took off her apron.

'Never you worry,' she told the girl. 'I'll soon be back, and then you can talk to Mrs Meldrum.'

She put on her coat and set off down the road. What an odd situation!

Well, there won't be much work done today, she told herself. That's for certain!

'Hello, Jess! Come away in.'

The housekeeper stood on the doorstep, looking slightly flustered – her coat was buttoned up anyhow, and her face was troubled.

'I'm sorry to disturb you, Miss Marian, but could you come up to the farm, you and your mother?'

'Well, yes, of course we will, but what's the matter? Is there something wrong?'

The housekeeper shook her head.

'There's nothing wrong exactly. But we'd be glad of your help – that is, Mr Holt asked.'

Marian stiffened slightly. But then she looked at Jess – kind, warm-hearted Jess, who would do anything to help someone in trouble.

'It's a visitor, wanting to see your mother.'

Marian was puzzled, but she could see Jess was reluctant to say more.

92

'Of course we'll come, right away.'

Jess was relieved when Marian and her mother readily agreed.

'Elspeth!' Betsy called up the stairs. 'We're going up to the farm.'

The girl came jumping down the stairs two at a time.

'I'll come, too! I want to talk to Mr Holt.'

'No, Elspeth, not just now, dear.' Jess spoke firmly. 'Someone wants to see your mother.'

Elspeth was a little put out, but nodded and went back upstairs.

'Can you tell us what's happened?' Marian asked as they made their way up the garden path, between rose bushes still heavy with the night's rain. 'Who is it that wants to see Mother so urgently?'

'It's a girl ... wanting to speak to your mother particularly.'

Jess was reluctant to say more. She would leave it to Mr Holt to explain the circumstances of the girl's arrival.

'Well, you should have just sent her down to us,' Betsy scolded mildly. 'We're always pleased to have visitors.'

But Marian was puzzled. What was wrong? Jess had looked as if she was about to say something, then stopped.

All the way up to the house, Jess was unusually silent, and Marian felt a sense of foreboding. This was most unlike Jess. Normally she'd be bursting with news of her comings and goings. And she wasn't the type to over-dramatise things.

'You'll excuse the kitchen,' Jess said when they reached the farmhouse. 'I know it's the middle of the morning but Mr Holt was out in the fields early and breakfast was late—'

'This is kind of you to come.' Paul Holt met them at the door. 'We are in some difficulty here. There is a young lady…' He explained briefly the girl's arrival in the middle of the night.

'My goodness!' Betsy was astonished. 'The poor thing!'

'She's asking for you, Mrs Meldrum, and no-one else. She says that she has to speak to you.'

'To me? But why?' Betsy was bewildered.

'She's in the kitchen. Won't you come in?'

He gave a little nod to Marian, and she followed her mother into the kitchen.

The big farm kitchen was all too familiar. Marian remembered it as a child and the comfort of winter afternoons spent helping Jess to roll out pastry and make scones. There had always been a bright fire in the range, and the homely smell of a good broth simmering on the stove.

But now was no time for memories. She stopped when she saw the white-faced girl sitting at the old kitchen table.

'Simone,' Paul said kindly, 'this is Mrs Meldrum, and her daughter, Miss Marian Meldrum.' He glanced at Marian, then back to the girl. 'This is Simone – we don't know her surname.'

The young woman rose, and stood a little unsteadily, holding on to the table for support.

'Please sit down, my dear.' Betsy's tone was kindly and full of concern. She could see how weak and exhausted Simone was, and realised the girl was making a great effort.

Betsy herself took a chair at the table while Marian remained standing.

Paul stood by the door, his eyes on the little group, and Jess, for something to do, picked up the kettle and filled it at the sink.

'Well, I'm here now...' Betsy began.

Simone nodded. Marian noticed that she clutched a little black case tightly to her, as if it contained something very precious.

'What is it, my dear?' Betsy probed gently.

Simone gave a deep sigh.

'Madame Meldrum...' Her voice was barely above a whisper. 'Your son, William...'

'My son was killed in the war.' Betsy's tone was flat. A stranger would have thought she was resigned to the loss, but only Marian knew how her mother still grieved.

'Your son, William...' the girl went on. And then as if she was making a great effort, she spoke quietly.

'I am William's wife.'

There was almost complete silence in the room, broken only by a little gasp from Jess.

'No,' Betsy said, her voice strained. 'No, it's not possible.'

Slowly, Simone removed a chain from her neck with a small key attached. She opened the case and took out some documents.

'*Regarde* – I have some papers. And a photograph.'

'Let me see.' Marian moved forward and picked up the documents.

She looked at them closely, then took up the photograph, gazing at it even more intently.

Betsy sat very still, as if she couldn't take in what Simone had just said.

The only sound in the room was the ticking of the clock on the mantelpiece.

'Mother,' Marian said, putting her arm

around Betsy. 'There is a marriage certificate. And a photo of William in uniform. I think what she says must be true. She *is* William's wife.'

Chapter Four

'I don't believe it!' Betsy could hardly get the words out. Her eyes were fixed on Simone's ashen face.

'It's true, Mother,' Marian said gently, looking up from the documents the girl had brought with her. 'The proof is here.'

'But William...' Betsy began, then fell silent.

'I know it's hard to take in,' Marian said gently.

'How can you be so calm?' Anguished, Betsy turned to face her daughter as if they were the only two people in the room.

Marian said nothing, but sat down beside her mother and put her hand over Betsy's. Her mother's wedding ring was so thin and worn it was only a narrow band of gold.

Marian thought rapidly. Her mother needed time to think, to accept this bombshell. She'd been so brave up till now. After William's death, Betsy had carried on, quietly, steadfastly. This would only re-open the wounds.

Marian glanced round the kitchen. Simone still sat at the big table, while Jess was being tactful, busying herself making tea. Paul Holt stood by the window.

I wonder what he's making of it all, Marian thought ruefully. I don't suppose this sort of thing happens in *his* family.

Hastily, she turned her thoughts back to her mother, her mind racing. What can we do? Where will Simone stay? The questions buzzed around in her head...

Still Betsy said nothing, but she sipped the tea Jess gave her, shivering a little, and warming her hands around the cup.

Marian turned to Paul.

'I'm sorry about this,' she said in a matter-of-fact way. 'We won't stay long, I promise. You must have lots of things to see to. You won't want us here.'

How cool she was, Paul thought. How capable!

'There is no hurry,' he assured her.

What on earth did one say to people in such a situation?

'You're not disturbing me in the least,' he went on, a little gruffly. 'Please stay...'

He stopped suddenly, his face reddening.

'I think,' Jess put in, 'that what Mr Holt means to say is, if Miss Simone–' maybe she *was* William's wife, but she couldn't bring herself to say Mrs Meldrum '–if she'd like to stay here, there's plenty of room. Till you've sorted things out, that is.'

'Thank you, Jess.' Marian gave her an affectionate smile.

Betsy still hadn't spoken to Simone, but was staring at her, almost in disbelief.

Marian knew how her mother must be feeling – stunned, unnerved, torn apart by grief for William. And yet this girl was the last person here who had seen William alive...

There were so many questions to ask, but not now. And not in front of Paul Holt. Marian's face flushed, and she brushed a strand of hair from her forehead.

'Simone,' she said gently, 'this has been a great shock to my mother. I'm sure you understand.'

The girl nodded.

'I am sorry you are upset, *Madame*. I understand,' she said haltingly.

Betsy raised her head and looked across the table at the thin white-faced girl with huge dark eyes.

Jess refilled the cups, and offered round a plate of scones. Usually, Marian enjoyed Jess's scones, spread with farm butter and strawberry jam. But today, she shook her head.

Betsy and Simone both declined, though the French girl drank her second cup thirstily.

'Well–' Paul broke the silence. 'If there's nothing I can do... I mean, I'd be very glad ... any help you want.'

'We're most grateful, Mr Holt.' Marian fixed her clear blue eyes on his face. 'But it won't be necessary. We'll manage.'

At the sound of a car drawing up outside, they all turned towards the door, as if grateful for any interruption.

'It's the doctor!' Jess said.

'Hello there.' Robert stopped in the doorway, surprised to see Marian and her mother. 'Good morning, Mrs Meldrum. Hello, Marian.' He turned to Simone. 'And how's my patient this morning?'

Bien, thank you...' Simone murmured.

'She's much better, Doctor,' Jess said briskly. 'But it's good of you to call.'

'Did you sleep well?' Robert asked, setting his bag down on the table.

'Thank you.' Simone nodded again.

'Good.' Robert turned enquiringly towards Paul, then Marian.

Robert – good, kind, dependable Robert,

she thought. He looked so solid and normal in the midst of this strange situation. He would know what to do. He always did.

She willed herself to speak as calmly as she could.

'Robert, Simone asked Mother and me to come up here so she could tell us...' She paused. 'It seems... I mean, that is... Simone was married to my brother, William.' She paused again. 'During the war, before he went off to the Front.'

Robert glanced round the little group.

'We don't know much more,' Marian said hastily. 'But I'm sure Simone will tell us in time.'

She smiled at the girl, who gave her a tremulous half smile in return.

The young doctor quickly summed up the situation. Clearing a place at the table, he sat down in the chair beside Betsy and put his hand over hers.

'I'm sure this has been a great surprise – a shock to you, Mrs Meldrum,' he said in a matter-of-fact way.

Hearing his kindly tones, Betsy turned to him, and suddenly tears welled up in her eyes.

'It's a great deal to take in, I know,' Robert said gently. 'And I see Jess has made a cup of tea – quite the best thing.'

He talked on in an even tone of voice and soon Betsy began to recover herself.

Marian turned to Paul.

'We're very grateful to you, Mr Holt,' she said. 'But I think perhaps we ought to go home now.'

'The young lady is welcome to stay here,' Paul said, a little stiffly. 'We have plenty of room.'

'Thank you,' Marian said. 'But we won't presume any longer. If Simone is feeling well enough–' she looked enquiringly at Robert '–would she be able to come home with us?'

For the first time, she spoke directly to Simone, slowly, because she wasn't sure how much the girl understood.

'Would you like to come with us to our cottage? My mother and I and my young sister – we live not far way. We will be glad to welcome you.'

Paul, glancing at her, noticed a slight flush on her cheek and realised what an effort her words had been. It couldn't be easy to be welcoming in such circumstances.

'Thank you.' Simone raised her eyes to Marian's. 'That is very kind of you.'

'Then that's agreed,' Robert said. 'It's not

far, but I've got the car outside, and I'll be glad to run you down to the cottage.'

'Thank you, Robert,' Betsy said as he helped her to her feet.

'I'll get your things,' Jess told Simone. 'I've dried some of your clothes – they're on the fireguard.' She bustled about as she spoke.

'You have all been so kind to me.' Simone spoke slowly. 'Thank you.'

As the small group made their way out into the yard, Marian hung back for a moment.

'We're very grateful,' she said simply to Paul. 'I realise you have quite enough to do without this. Thank you.'

'There's no need,' he said again, rather formally.

'Marian,' he went on, and then stopped, embarrassed at having used her first name. 'Will you be all right, you and your mother?'

She paused, looking directly at him with that frank gaze.

'I don't know,' she said simply, then left.

Paul gazed after her for a moment, then picked up the letters and documents he needed. There was work waiting for him.

On the short journey down to the cottage, Robert chattered evenly about the weather.

'If it's your first visit to Scotland, you're seeing it at its best.'

He glanced at Simone as they drove along the lane with its hedgerows of dog roses and pink campion, and honeysuckle scrambling over the walls that bordered the field.

Betsy was still silent and he caught her eye.

'I'll come in and see how you are tomorrow.'

She smiled her thanks.

When they reached the cottage, he helped first Betsy, then Simone, out.

'I'll see you tomorrow,' he promised Marian, as he turned to go back to the car. 'I'd better be off on my rounds now.'

Betsy opened the door.

'Come in,' she invited Simone. 'It's not a very big house, but it's our home now. And...' She paused. 'You are very welcome.'

'Mother! Where have you been? You've been ages...' Elspeth burst into the kitchen, then stopped at the door, her voice trailing away. 'Oh...'

She stared at Simone and then at Marian. 'Who...? I mean...'

Marian moved towards her sister.

'Simone, this is my young sister, Elspeth. Elspeth, this is Simone.'

'How do you do,' Elspeth said politely, looking puzzled.

'Mother, why don't you and Simone sit here for a little, while Elspeth and I get Simone's room ready?' Marian suggested. 'She can have my room. You'll help me, won't you, Elspeth?'

Without waiting for a reply, she gently pushed her sister out of the room.

Bewildered, Elspeth sat down on the old Bentwood chair by the window in Marian's room.

'What's going on?' she demanded.

'There's a spare bed. I'll put it up in your room. For the moment, anyway,' Marian said briskly. Then, explaining as clearly as she could, she told her sister everything.

'And so,' she finished, 'we thought it best if she came back here with us.'

Elspeth was silent for a moment or two.

'I don't understand...' she said at last.

'Nor do I,' Marian confessed. 'There's still a great deal to talk about. But she's pretty tired, still, and she needs to rest.

'Come on, let's get the room ready, and then we'll go downstairs.'

In the kitchen, Betsy and Simone sat opposite each other, not speaking. Obviously, language was a problem.

'We've made the bed,' Marian announced as cheerfully as she could, 'and the room is ready for you, Simone, if you want to rest.'

Simone raised her dark eyes to Marian's and smiled.

'You are all so good,' she said haltingly. 'I thank you.'

'Do you speak much English?' Marian asked the girl.

Simone shook her head.

'A little. Not much. I did not learn.'

'Simone, we have many questions to ask,' Marian said, as kindly as she could. 'We want to know all about you – and William. Can you tell us in English?'

'I will try,' the girl said helplessly. 'William and I...'

'Yes?' Marian's tone was gentle and encouraging.

'Long time ... we ... he is ... he was soldier...' Her voice trailed away.

Marian and Betsy waited patiently, but the girl screwed her handkerchief into a ball and pressed it to her mouth.

'You're tired,' Marian said kindly. 'Perhaps it's all too much just now ... but you understand we do need to know?'

'I want to tell you,' Simone said. 'I do not speak English well, but...'

'And I don't speak French very fluently,' Marian said cheerfully, 'but between us we'll manage!'

Marian thought she would remember all her life the sounds of that morning – a sheepdog barking down the lane, the rustle of the beech hedge – as Simone unfolded her tale of love and loss.

She had come to know William when he was billeted at her uncle's farm. Simone went to visit her cousins, and immediately the young Scotsman began to pay her special attention.

One evening, he'd offered to see her home, and soon after he had asked her father's permission to walk out with her.

Marian remembered fondly how William, so lively and often boisterous, had been shy and tongue-tied with girls. How he would blush scarlet if he had to ask a girl for a dance, or suddenly met one of Marian's friends in the village.

He must, she thought, have fallen immediately in love with Simone to be so determined on marriage.

From then on, Simone's voice trembled. She recovered herself to explain they had been married quickly, because William knew he was likely to be called to the Front.

They had been married twice, once in a civil ceremony and once in church, according to the French custom.

'And then?' Marian asked.

William had been called to the Front with his regiment, after only a week or two of married life. Simone had heard nothing more – until two friends of his arrived in the village and told her of his death.

'But why?' Betsy asked. She had been silent up till now. '*Why* didn't he tell us he was married?'

'I'll try to find out.' Marian recognised the anguish in her mother's voice.

She put the question, in halting French, to Simone.

The girl burst into a torrent of speech.

'But he *did* write! He wrote a few days after we were married. He wanted you to know. He wanted to bring me to meet you after the war. And he said...' Her voice broke. 'If he ... if he didn't come back, you would look after me.'

There was a silence.

'We didn't receive his letter...' Betsy said at last.

Marian immediately translated this.

'But I thought...'

'You poor girl,' Betsy said suddenly. 'What

must you have thought of us? You must have believed we were angry. As if we would be!'

Marian tried lamely to put this into French. She reached across the table, taking Simone's hands in hers.

'I thought you did not want to meet me, perhaps...'

Marian tried to explain.

'In wartime, letters often went missing. It must have been lost in the post from France. But it—' she paused, wondering how to put it '—it's good to meet you at last. But why did you not come to see us before, or perhaps write again?'

'We are proud people, my family,' the girl said with some dignity. 'At first I thought, if they do not want me, I do not write! And then my father became ill. We had a little shop – a grocer's shop. I helped my father. Then, when he was very ill, I looked after the shop myself.' She paused. 'You understand?'

'Please, go on,' Marian prompted.

'I could not leave him to go to Scotland. And then, after five years, my father died.'

'I'm sorry,' Betsy murmured, her eyes on Simone's face.

'I thought, now I will sell the shop. I do not wish to stay in the village. My mother, she, too, is dead. But I have uncle, aunt,

110

cousins. They say, you must stay. Here is your home.' She spread her hands out wide.

'I do not know what to do. So I ask *le curé* – the priest. "You must write to your husband's family. Tell them about your marriage," he told me.

'"But it is long time ago," I say.

'"No matter," he says. "You must tell them. Write. I help you."

'I say, "no."' Simone drew a deep breath. '"I will go and visit William's family. Now my father is dead, I am alone."

'The priest, he said, "Is that wise? It will be a..."'

'Shock?' Marian put in.

Simone nodded.

'A shock to them.'

'That's true.' Marian gave a faint smile. 'It certainly was a shock.'

'I am sorry,' Simone said. 'But I thought – a letter, it is cold. I want to go myself to tell them about William.'

'And we're glad you did,' Betsy said warmly.

'It must have been very difficult, to make the journey,' Marian said sympathetically.

'Yes, I had not travelled so far before.' Simone sighed. 'But the good priest, he helped me. He wrote to the Sisters in

London. When I came there, they met me. I stayed at the convent, and then they took me to the train. They were all kind to me.

'I knew just your name, *Madame,* and the farm. But I knew I would find you.'

'I'm glad you came ... Simone.' Betsy wiped her eyes.

The next day, Robert called in, just as he'd promised. Marian felt a sense of relief wash over her. Things always seemed easier when Robert was around.

'And how are you this morning?' He sat down beside Simone.

'Well, I don't think you need me any more,' he said after a few minutes. 'Rest quietly for a few days – you'll soon be back to normal. No, thanks.' He shook his head at Betsy's offer of a cup of tea. 'I must be on my way. I've quite a list today.'

'We've heard Simone's account,' Marian explained as she walked with him to the car. 'How she and William met, and married, and why she's taken so long to get in touch. I think it's going to be all right.'

'I'm glad,' he said warmly. 'It's better for your mother if matters are cleared up right away.

'Better for you, too,' he went on. 'But I can see you're coping, as always. Some time, if you want to tell me about it, I'd be glad to listen – and help if I can. But I know it's a private matter.'

'Not private from you,' Marian said quickly. 'You're one of our oldest friends. I'll tell you when you've got more time.'

'Let me know if I can help,' he repeated. 'Any time.' As he drove off, he looked back at her standing there waving, the breeze ruffling her hair.

'One of our oldest friends,' he said to himself, and gave a rueful smile as he rounded the bend in the lane.

That evening, after tea, the three women sat quietly together. Elspeth had gone to visit a friend. Betsy was turning the heel of a stocking she was knitting, while Marian was mending a tear in a sheet.

Simone watched her for a little while.

'Please, I can help you?' she offered.

'Thank you.'

Gladly, Marian handed over the mending, and went to sit on the window seat.

When at last she went to bed that evening, her head was buzzing with the events of the past few days. But oddly, uppermost in her mind was a conversation she'd had with Simone just after tea, as they washed the dishes together.

'Doctor Robert – he is very kind,' the girl had said.

'Indeed he is,' Marian had said warmly.

'You and he, you are, how do you say it – affianced?'

'Oh, good heavens, no!' Marian had protested. But the conversation remained in her mind.

How odd! What a strange – no, impossible idea, she thought as she drifted off to sleep.

Dear Sarah, Paul wrote. *It has been a very eventful time…*

It was difficult to find a spare moment to write, so much had happened in the past few days. Sarah, he knew, would be fascinated to hear about the circumstances of Simone's arrival.

A few days ago, he continued, *there was a ring at the doorbell…*

He broke off, and threw down his pen as the doorbell pealed. There was always, he thought irritably, *some* interruption in this place.

'May I come in for a moment?'

Marian stood on the doorstep. It had been a warm day and she looked hot and tired.

Paul immediately forgot that he'd been interrupted.

114

'It's good to see you,' he said. 'Please, come in.'

'I hope you don't mind my calling.' Marian hesitated. 'You're probably just relaxing after a hard day's work.'

'How are things going?' he asked. 'Your...' He was about to say 'sister-in-law', but didn't know whether this was quite appropriate. 'Simone. Is she all right? And your mother?'

'Yes, thanks.' Marian gave a little sigh. 'We're managing.'

'Look, do come in and sit down.' He led the way into the room that was now his office.

'I see I'm interrupting – again,' Marian couldn't help adding, but her words had no visible effect on Paul.

'It doesn't matter in the least. What can I do to help you?'

'I wondered...' Marian began in a rush. 'We haven't a lot of space in the cottage at the moment. Elspeth's desperate to keep up her piano practise, and she's really quite good, but you see...'

She took a deep breath.

'There doesn't seem to be anywhere we can put a piano at the moment. The parlour is still full of furniture. We'll need to get rid of some of it...'

She paused, aware she was talking far too much. Why does this man always look so superior, she wondered. He makes me feel so foolish!

'Of course,' Paul said, 'it's perfectly all right if Elspeth wants to come and practise here. I'm out most of the time, but Jess is always in. She won't be disturbing anyone.'

'Oh,' Marian said. 'You've taken the wind out of my sails! All the way up the lane, I've been rehearsing my words, wondering what I'd do if you refused.' She gave a nervous little laugh.

'Did you really think I'd say no?' Paul asked.

'I thought you might,' Marian admitted.

'Surely I'm not as forbidding as all that?'

'Well, no.' Marian was embarrassed again. 'But it is a lot to ask.'

Paul got up from his chair and stood leaning against the desk and smiling across at her.

'I'm only too glad to help you – and your family. Tell Elspeth she's welcome to come and practise here.'

'Thank you.' Marian got to her feet. 'I'm sorry I've disturbed you. But thank you again... I'd better go.'

'No, please stay a moment,' Paul began, but she was off down the stairs and out of the door.

He was thoughtful as he returned to his desk. She was hard to get to know, he told himself, but in time, perhaps...

After a few minutes, he began his letter again. What a lot had happened since he last wrote to Sarah. Should he tell her how things were going on the farm? The truth? That it was all harder work then he'd expected?

He had good help in Geordie and Bob, but it had been a difficult summer. The weather had been poor, and some of the rasps hadn't done well. Maybe he'd replace them with other varieties that would stand a lot of rain.

And, he had to admit, he was disappointed that Sergeant Fordyce hadn't taken up his offer.

Paul leaned back in his chair. After a hectic week, he could at least relax for an hour, even if worries came crowding in.

Then the doorbell rang again and he rose to answer it.

'I'm sorry to bother you, sir,' Geordie began apologetically.

'Come in.' Paul knew Geordie wouldn't

have come up to the house in the evening unless something important had happened.

Geordie hesitated.

'I don't like to trouble you,' he said again, 'but it's the pickers.'

Paul groaned inwardly, but nodded at Geordie to continue.

'There's been a fight!' Geordie said dramatically.

'What happened, Geordie? Who started it?'

'One of the men from the huts at Wester Essendy. A crowd of them went off to the pictures at Coupar Angus. They stopped at the pub for a drink, and this man – Murdo MacLean's his name – got into a fight.'

He paused for breath.

'His pals took him back to the camp, but he was still bawling and fighting. He's past listening to reason.'

'I'll come and sort it out,' Paul said coolly, sighing inwardly.

Later on, having calmed things down and reassured Murdo's tearful wife that he wouldn't be sacked, Paul announced he'd be back to talk to the man when he was sober.

'But it can't happen again,' he told Murdo's wife firmly. The troublemaker was now fast asleep and snoring.

'Any more of this and he's finished.'

'Thank you, mister.' He felt sorry for the wife; she was thin and shabbily dressed, with greying hair drawn back into a bun. From the ages of the children clustered around her, Paul guessed she couldn't be more than forty or so, but she looked a great deal older.

Paul began to trudge back to the farmhouse. By now it was getting dark. It had been a long day and he'd be glad to turn in.

As he approached the lane that led to the Meldrums' cottage, he thought he heard someone coming along the path.

One of the pickers? But it was out of their way ... was someone hanging around the cottage? He grasped his stick, prepared to challenge an intruder.

'It's you!'

'You gave me quite a surprise!'

'I thought it might be an intruder!'

Marian laughed.

'I live here, remember?' She looked a little shamefaced. 'I felt – well, I just wanted some time to myself.'

'In that case,' Paul said, 'I'm sorry if I disturbed you.'

'No,' she put in hastily, 'it's all right, really.'

There was a small silence between them

before he spoke.

'Do you mind if I walk back with you – to see you safely home? I promise I won't talk if you'd rather we didn't.'

Marian smiled, and he thought how different she was when she wasn't being angry or defensive.

'Thank you. I'd be glad of your company. And, please do talk if you want – I don't mean to be that solitary.'

They turned and made their way back along the lane.

'I hope things work out with your sister-in-law,' he said.

'I hope so, too,' Marian agreed thoughtfully. 'It's early to tell, but she seems to fit in, somehow. And Mother likes her, I can tell.' To her astonishment, she found herself telling Paul all about Simone.

He listened, saying very little.

'I can't think why I'm telling you all this,' Marian said with a little laugh. 'It can't really be of interest to you.'

'But of course it is,' he protested. 'I'll do anything I can to help you – you know that.'

She stopped and turned to him, and for a moment they stood, looking at each other with sudden understanding.

'I think,' he continued slowly, 'that you've

done a wonderful job – not just welcoming Simone, but everything – the farm, keeping things going after your brother...' His voice trailed off. 'I admire the way you've coped,' he said firmly.

Marian was suddenly aware that they were chatting like two people who had known each other for ages. She realised to her astonishment that this man wasn't standoffish or haughty at all! She'd thought him rather remote – distant somehow. Now she found she was having to revise her opinion...

'I'd like us to be friends,' Paul said as if sensing her thoughts. 'I feel I've come in, taken over your home – I don't want there to be any bad feeling between us.'

'There won't be,' Marian said softly.

'I'm glad about that.'

Suddenly, Marian tripped over a stone on the path, and he grasped her elbow to keep her from falling.

'Careful! Are you all right?'

'Yes, quite all right.' She smiled at him again. He kept hold of her arm as they went on up the lane, and somehow it felt easy and natural that they should be walking together.

'I'm glad I met you,' he said after a silence. 'You see – Marian – I'd like your advice.'

121

'Oh?' She was puzzled.

'It's about the pickers. I've been sorting out some trouble tonight.' He explained briefly what had happened.

'They're a decent enough crowd, and I'm sure this kind of thing doesn't happen often. But it made me think – I don't really have much to do with the day-to-day running of the berry fields.'

He warmed to his subject, talking animatedly.

'Geordie – well, he's very much my right-hand man, but he's getting on in years. I should oversee things – paying out the wages and seeing to the accommodation – but I just don't have the time! What with running the farm, getting the fruit to the trains and dealing with accounts... Tell me, how did you manage? Did you supervise the pickers yourself? I'd welcome your advice...'

He turned to face her.

'It really was lucky we happened to meet tonight.'

'Yes, wasn't it?' Marian's tone was suddenly chilly. So that was why he was so pleasant – he needed to pick her brains about organising the farm! She felt foolish and totally misled. He wasn't interested in getting to know her at all.

'I'm sure,' she continued coolly, 'that you don't need my advice. You're quite capable of organising the pickers yourself.'

They had reached the cottage gate by now.

'Good night, Mr Holt. And thank you for seeing me home.' She turned away and went indoors without looking back.

Paul turned away, perplexed. What was the matter? They'd been talking in such a pleasant way, but then suddenly she'd become chilly and distant.

He shrugged. If that was the way she wanted it, he wouldn't try again to be friends.

On the way up the lane, he thought about Marian. If only she'd been willing to help and advise. Surely anyone would have been flattered to have been asked about their expert knowledge? The woman was impossible, and besides, he had more than enough to worry about.

Back home, he picked up the letter he'd been writing to his sister. 'Don't give up,' he could hear her saying. No wonder so many people turned to Sarah – she was so sensible, so level-headed.

Now Paul realised he needed more help in running the farm. He needed someone like

Sergeant Fordyce. He decided to go to see him in person, find out what was wrong and, somehow, make him change his mind.

'What a hive of industry!' Robert paused in the doorway at the scene before him.

Simone was preparing vegetables at the kitchen table, while Betsy was busy at the kitchen sink. In a quiet corner, Marian was listening to young Dougie read.

The doctor produced a couple of pennies.

'I hear you're a grand reader, Dougie. Here, buy yourself some sweets.'

Dougie's eyes shone.

'Can I go now, miss?'

'Oh, all right.' Marian laughed. 'Off you go.'

She turned to Robert.

'He comes up here in the dinner break. It's gratifying to see how much he's learned.'

Betsy wiped her hands.

'Would you like a cup of tea, Robert?'

The young man shook his head.

'I just looked in on my way to the Lawsons. I've a call there. I don't need to ask if all's well here. You seem much better,' he told Simone.

She smiled up at him. 'I am well ... now. Betsy and Marian have been so kind to me.

Elspeth, too. But I must not – how do you say – stay too long. I impose.'

'Nonsense,' Betsy said firmly. 'We're glad to have you.'

'And look at how Mother keeps her hard at work,' Marian said slyly, indicating the basin of carrots. 'She never stops!'

'Now you are joking, I think!' Simone laughed.

'Well, I'm glad to see you're so much better.' Robert smiled. 'And now I'll be on my way. Perhaps I'll see you later, Marian? Maybe a walk this evening?'

Marian hesitated.

'Perhaps.' She followed Robert to the door and waved as he climbed into his car.

It was such a lovely day... It would be pleasant, Marian thought, to have someone to share it.

She had been standing at the door for a few minutes, enjoying the fresh breeze, when her senses were suddenly alert. Surely she was mistaken? It couldn't be smoke... No-one was burning stubble yet, and it was too early for autumn bonfires.

And yet – she was almost certain! As she looked towards the farm, she was sure she could see a plume of smoke.

And was that the crackle of flames – or

was she imagining it? Suddenly, she was certain. There was a fire – and it was up at the farm!

Chapter Five

'It's a fire, miss! In the far field! It'll spread to the rasp fields – everything's tinder dry!'

Geordie had met Marian as she reached the farmhouse.

'I'll telephone the fire brigade. Geordie, get as many pickers as you can, and buckets. There's a tap in the yard by the barn.'

Geordie turned back to the fields, and Marian rushed into the farmhouse to pick up the telephone in the hall. Thank goodness they'd decided to have it installed, just two years ago. She gave an urgent message to the operator, then decided quickly what must be done.

Down in the big field, she could see flames crackling and smoke drifting towards the rows of berries. There were plenty of buckets in the barn ... until the firemen arrived, everyone available would be needed for the chain.

Marian felt herself near panic. Would there be time to save the berryfields? Almost at once about half a dozen lads, led by Dougie

Mackay, came racing into the yard. And at that moment, she heard the sound of a car approaching.

Robert jumped out.

'I saw the smoke from the road.' He wasted no time in pulling off his jacket. 'Come on, lads!' He filled a bucket and passed it to the first boy.

Marian hunted desperately for more containers. In the field, Bob was trying to contain the blaze.

'Hurry! We need more people!'

Some of the women arrived, skirts kilted up to their knees, and began passing buckets from one to another. Down in the field, Marian could hear the ominous crackle of the flames.

Only one man – Marian recognised him as Murdo – hung back. She didn't know his surname, but Bob and Geordie had spoken of him, pointing him out as a surly type who spent a lot of time in the local pubs.

For now, Marian paid him no attention. There were plenty of willing helpers.

It was only ten minutes or so, but it seemed much longer before the firemen arrived.

'A bit longer and it would have spread to the fields,' they remarked, as they uncoiled hoses and set about the job with professional skill.

Within a short time, the panic was over. Marian, feeling drained, watched as the firemen prepared to leave.

Robert, who'd handed out buckets and helped direct the pickers, reached for his jacket.

'Any idea how it started?' he asked the firemen.

'It's bone dry, sir. Could have been anything – maybe a cigarette end...'

The fireman turned to Marian.

'Keep an eye on it, miss, will you? Call us if you've any problems.'

'It's not my farm any more,' Marian said defensively. 'It belongs to Mr Holt now.'

'Oh? Is he here?'

'He's gone to Glasgow for the day,' Bob said quickly. 'He won't be back till late.'

Marian thanked the firemen and the pickers.

'You've done a grand job. You probably saved the berryfield.'

They beamed back at her – most of the pickers knew Marian and liked her.

'Come on.' Robert took her by the arm. 'I'll clean up, then set off on my rounds again. I'll call in tonight on my way home.'

He was angry with Paul Holt. *He* was the land-owner! Marian shouldn't have had to cope with all this!

As Robert drove off, he knew that he had to speak to Marian. Several times, he had tried to tell her of his feelings – but now, looking at her white, exhausted face, he knew all he wanted to do was protect her and care for her.

There was, he realised, no-one else quite like Marian – and he had known it for a long time.

It was late afternoon before he returned to the cottage and found her sitting outside, a book in her hand.

'Am I disturbing you?'

'Not at all.' Marian closed the book and smiled at him. 'I was glad of your help today, Robert. I daren't think what might have happened…'

'Still no sign of Paul Holt, I presume?' Robert's tone was acid.

'None at all. What Mr Holt does is his own affair. If he chooses to go off and leave the farm…' Her voice trailed off.

'He ought to be very grateful to you.'

Marian shrugged.

Suddenly, Robert leaned forward and took

her hand.

'Marian, this may not be the right time, or the place, but I can't wait any longer. You know I love you – I've loved you for years. And I want to look after you, to care for you. There's nothing I want more…'

'I know…' his voice was not quite steady. '…I could make you happy. Marian, will you marry me?'

'Oh, Robert.' Gently, Marian drew her hand away. 'I didn't know. You've taken me by surprise…'

'Say yes,' he prompted gently. 'Please.'

There was a long pause. In the silence between them, Marian could hear the insistent notes of a song thrush in the hedge at the end of the garden.

'I wish I could say yes,' she murmured at last. 'But I honestly don't know.'

'I've rushed things a bit.' He put his hand over hers. 'But will you promise you'll think it over? I'm prepared to wait.'

'I promise you that, Robert. Just give me a little time…'

Blissfully unaware of recent events at the farm, Paul drew a deep breath, then coughed.

After all these months in the clear pure air

of Perthshire, he'd almost forgotten what it was like in the city: the smoke billowing from the chimneys, the soot-encrusted buildings, the noise of the trams and so many people scurrying past.

Paul had memorised Sergeant Fordyce's address and found it without too much difficulty.

He rapped at the door on the second floor of a grey tenement building, noticing that the doorknocker was polished and gleaming. He waited for a few minutes, wondering whether this was a bad time to call. The sergeant was probably out at work. But would his wife – if there was a wife – be at home?

He was just about to give up when he heard footsteps, and the door opened.

'Captain Holt! Well, this is a surprise!'

There was no mistaking the sergeant's pleasure at seeing him as he shook Paul warmly by the hand.

'Come away in, sir, and tell me what brings you here.'

He was still the same Sergeant Fordyce – bright-eyed, and with a crisp way of speaking. Fairly short in stature, he held himself erect so that he had a certain presence. His moustache was neatly trimmed and his appearance tidy – though Paul couldn't help noticing that the cuffs of his jacket were frayed.

'Come in!' the sergeant repeated.

Paul found himself in a small kitchen. There was a bright fire in the grate, and soup bubbling on the stove.

'I hope I'm not disturbing you?' he said.

'No, indeed. Please, take a chair.' The sergeant moved a pair of boots which he had been cleaning.

'You see–' he'd noticed Paul's glance '–I try to keep up standards, just as we always did, eh, sir?'

Paul nodded, glancing round the room. It was sparsely furnished, but spotlessly clean.

'You'll take a cup of tea, sir?'

Paul nodded.

The sergeant, for the first time, seemed a little ill at ease. He filled the kettle at the sink and set out two cups, milk and sugar.

'So, how are you, sir?' the sergeant asked, noticing how Paul's hand trembled as he put down his cup.

'I'm fine...' Paul paused. 'Most of the time,' he added, looking directly at his old friend.

'I know.' The sergeant paused. 'But you're looking grand, sir.'

'I felt such a fraud,' Paul said quietly, as if to himself. 'Invalided home when there was nothing much the matter with me.'

'Nothing much the matter!' The sergeant scoffed. 'You were injured, sir, and badly, too. And you know you could have saved your own skin and left that poor lad in the trench. But you didn't.'

Paul went on to tell him about the rift with his family. He realised that the sergeant wasn't in work – if he was, he wouldn't be at home at this time of day.

'I remember you said you worked on a farm up near Inverness,' Paul remarked. 'It's a lovely place I've got, near Blairgowrie. I was surprised when you turned my offer down. But maybe you've found something better?'

'I've nothing else.' The sergeant's voice was suddenly harsh. 'I haven't got a job, sir, and no prospect of one! I was a bit too proud to come straight out with it. To be honest with you, I didn't have the fare.'

'Jock, you knew I'd send the fare, and pay any expenses.'

'But I didn't want to admit that I was what they call one of the great unemployed. I was bitter, to tell you the truth, sir. Served King and country and started in a little job after the war.

'But when I got ill – the influenza – they fired me. All behind me now–' He shrugged.

'I've made up my mind, you see. They're wanting men to work on the farms in Canada – so that's where I'm going! As soon as I've got the money saved up, I'm off... You'll wish me luck, won't you, sir?'

Paul felt a shaft of disappointment.

'You've made up your mind?'

'That I have, sir. It's the wide open spaces for me!'

'Look, Jock, I need your help. I want someone who's good at handling people; someone with commonsense, who's not afraid of a bit of hard work.

'What I'm trying to say to you is...' Paul took a deep breath. 'I need *you* to help me. I can offer you a good job. We'd work well together, you know that. What do you say, Jock? Will you at least think it over?'

The sergeant paused.

'I don't need to think it over, sir,' he said in his deep voice. 'If you believe I can do the job, I'd be glad to accept your offer!'

Marian leaned back in her chair. Her mother was out visiting a friend and Elspeth had a music lesson. It was the first time

135

she'd had a moment to herself all day – and what a day it had been!

Partly, of course, that was because of Robert's proposal. What a time to choose to ask her! But that could wait. She pushed it to the back of her mind.

Suddenly, she felt herself shivering. Until now, she'd felt little reaction to the events of the day.

But now she felt restless and uneasy.

Suddenly, she rose, pulled on her jacket and put on a stout pair of shoes. She scribbled a note for Elspeth, in case her sister came home and found her gone. Then she set off up the lane to the farm to make sure everything was all right.

As she walked, she found herself wishing Robert was with her. It was odd how comforting it felt just to have him around.

She pushed open the door of the shed where the boxes were stored. A sudden movement made her start, and she whirled round.

There, watching her from the doorway, was Murdo! He was smoking a cigarette and leaning against the door.

Casually, almost insolently, he flicked the cigarette butt a few yards and ground it under his boot.

'So you've come to see these pickers aren't up to their devilry,' he began mockingly. 'Setting fire to berry fields and such...'

'It was *you*,' Marian said quietly as realisation dawned. 'You started the fire. And it wasn't an accident.'

He laughed.

'Someone was careless, miss! Just a dropped fag end. You're saying it was meant? Surely not.'

'Why?' Marian drew herself up and faced him.

'We don't want his sort round here,' the man said truculently. 'Playing at being a farmer, threatening to dock my wages, just because I'd had a drink...'

'So you wanted to get your own back ... you wanted to set the field alight, and hoped it would spread to the berries...'

'Maybe aye, maybe no...' The man didn't flinch.

'It was deliberate,' Marian said firmly. 'I know it.'

'But you'll not be able to prove it, will you?' Murdo said softly. Then he turned and strode off down the lane without looking back.

Jock Fordyce faced his new employer across the kitchen table.

'You're comfortable in the bothy, I hope,' Paul said anxiously.

'It's grand,' Sergeant Fordyce reassured him.

That first day had been easy enough. Paul had taken the sergeant up to the fields, and he'd met some of the pickers. He'd explained about the weighing and packing of the fruit, and the times the van went to the railway station.

'They shouldn't give you any trouble.' Paul waved towards the pickers. 'A good bunch for the most part.'

Geordie had told him all about the fire and how Marian and Robert had taken charge. He was grateful, of course, but glad that he could now leave things in Jock's capable hands.

Jock kept his doubts to himself. He'd already heard some of the women sniggering behind his back. Was it as easy to control a bunch of high-spirited females as it had been to keep his soldiers in order?

But there was no doubt in his mind that he was glad he'd made the move from Glasgow.

For the first few days, he was a bit tentative, finding his way, anxious not to appear too overbearing, but determined, too, not to seem weak.

'You've got to be firm,' Paul had warned him. 'See they pick the rows clean, otherwise there'll be a lot of waste.'

So when Bella Cushnie came down the dreel with her basket tied round her waist, he greeted her pleasantly.

'That's me done,' she said. 'I'll take another dreel now.'

'Just a minute.'

He wandered up the row, then back to stand beside her.

'There's plenty berries left. Away you go back and finish it off before you start a new row.'

She grumbled quietly but did as she was told. As he walked up the next dreel, he could hear her complaining bitterly.

'So he thinks he's somebody, that one, does he?'

'Fancy speaking to you like that, Bella. He has a nerve.'

Bella's chum, Jeannie, was only too eager to support her friend.

'Jumped-up wee nyaff!' Bella's voice rose.

Jock shrugged. There were bound to be problems at first. He knew some of the women imitated him, pretending to spring to attention.

It was just a pity he'd fallen out with the

ringleader – Bella by name, and obviously belligerent by nature!

Paul congratulated himself on finding such a good second-in-command and left Jock on his own the next day to attend to business in Perth. It had all worked out so well... Geordie and Bob approved of the sergeant, too – they liked his slow, quiet way of speaking, and thought he fitted in, listening to others, and saying very little himself.

Later that afternoon, Jock noticed a tall girl making her way towards the weighing shed.

'You must be Sergeant Fordyce,' she said, approaching him with a ready smile.

The sergeant paused in weighing up the baskets.

'I am that.'

Marian introduced herself.

'I hope you're liking our part of the world, after Glasgow.'

'It's grand.' He smiled back at her, and she realised she liked his honest, straightforward manner.

'I wanted to see Dougie – he comes to me to learn to read, and Mr Holt sometimes lets him away early. But I've something else to do today, so I'll not be at home.'

'Mr Holt's not here today, miss. He's gone to Perth.'

'Oh, well...' Marian was rather relieved not to find Paul at the berryfields. How much easier it was to talk to this solid, pleasant man.

'And how are you getting on?' she asked. 'They're a good lot, the pickers, if you can take their cheek! They come back year after year. I recall...'

She caught herself up. It didn't do to be remembering the past all the time.

'There are some grand workers – that man over there with the red hair. Murdo's his name – can't do enough to help.' Jock pointed to a man heaving a laden basket on to a cart.

Marian's breath caught in her throat.

'Get rid of him, Jock. That man's nothing but trouble! He was the one who started the fire.'

Without a word, Jock straightened his back and marched right over to Murdo MacLean...

When Paul came home, he heard the whole story – how Sergeant Fordyce had sent the sneering Murdo away with a flea in his ear.

'It was Marian who alerted me,' he

reminded Paul.

'Yes,' Paul said. 'I – we – owe her quite a lot. I'll make a point of thanking her.'

So he was in Marian's debt again! This was the second time she'd helped in a difficult situation – and Murdo could have created even more trouble if he'd been allowed to stay.

But why, he thought, did it have to be Marian? What a fool she must think him!

The next morning, there were more surprises in store for Paul.

'Your porridge is ready, Mr Holt.'

'Mmmm...' Paul hardly looked up from the letter he was reading.

What on earth was wrong with the man, Jess thought, with a touch of exasperation. Usually he was ready for his breakfast the minute he came in, and could hardly swallow it before he was out again into the fields.

'Your porridge will be cold,' she said again.

He came to with a start.

'I'm sorry, Jess, I was miles away. You're quite right. It's time I was getting on...'

He took a couple of spoonfuls, then looked over at Jess.

'I've had a letter this morning, from my sister. She's coming to stay. My father's been quite ill but he seems to be on the mend now. Sarah has helped to nurse him and would like a little break…'

'That's grand.' Jess beamed at him. 'It'll be nice for you to have her here for a while. When is she coming?'

'Well, er … this week. Saturday.'

'Saturday!'

'I know it's a bit sudden, Jess. I hope it wouldn't be too much of an imposition…'

'Away you go, it's no trouble at all.' Jess wiped her hands on her apron. 'There's the wee room above the porch – would that be all right? It gets all the sun, and I'll see it's well aired.'

'I'm very grateful.' Paul turned back to the letter with a wry smile, remembering Sarah as he'd last seen her – dark bobbed hair, short skirts, slim legs and high-heeled shoes! How would she like the quiet country life, he wondered?

When Saturday dawned, Paul drove down to the station to collect her.

'Paul!' Sarah left her luggage on the platform as she rushed forward to give him an affectionate hug.

'Welcome to Scotland!' Paul hugged her back.

Sarah looked round and drew a deep breath.

'I can hardly believe it – I'm actually here!'

All the way home, she chattered happily and as soon as Paul opened the car door, Sarah jumped out. And there was Jess, rosy-faced, in a fresh print apron, smiling in the doorway.

'Jess?' Sarah greeted the older woman warmly, then stood back. 'You're exactly as I imagined you!'

'Away you go.' Jess was slightly embarrassed, yet couldn't help responding to the warmth of this vivacious girl's greeting.

As the days passed, Paul was concerned that Sarah might be bored. Would she find enough to do, all on her own? After all, he was working. He didn't have time to drive her around the countryside, to provide entertainment.

'I can amuse myself even if it is the depths of the country,' Sarah laughed. 'Tell you what, I'll play these records I brought you. I'll be fine. You see to the farm as usual, Paul. Don't rush back!'

Each day when he returned, Sarah had something to tell him.

'It's such a friendly little place,' she decided as they sat in the parlour one evening. 'Do you all get together a lot?'

Paul shook his head.

'There isn't much time for socialising, I'm afraid.'

Sarah made a face.

'But you must relax sometimes, brother dear! I know...' she paused. 'Why don't you give a party for the end of the berry picking? You could ask all the pickers, and your friends. It'll be such fun!'

Marian was busy with her plans for the new term at school, and Betsy spent her time baking, sewing and knitting and visiting some of the older housebound folk in the village.

And Simone wondered just how *she* could spend the day...

What could she do? She knew she was skilled with her needle. Everyone said so. She'd made many first communion dresses for children in the village in France where she'd lived. Oh, she'd loved doing that. Many an afternoon she'd sat, carefully stitching...

A lump rose in her throat and she pushed the thought away.

Might there perhaps be a chance of work in one of the big houses, mending linen? Something to keep her busy, to keep her from thinking of – and then she laughed.

'How foolish I am! Of course there is a job for me here!'

Up in the berryfields, the sergeant was getting impatient. He'd already told off two of the women for idling.

'He's far too strict,' the others grumbled. 'Been in the Army and used to telling folk off. Well, he's not going to speak to me like that!'

Bella untied the basket from her waist.

'I'll find a job elsewhere.'

'Don't you be so daft,' the older one advised her. 'They pay well here.'

'Aye, you're right. I need the money.' Bella retied the string around her waist and began moving up the row again.

Well, that was a bad start to the day, Jock Fordyce thought. As he reached the bottom of the field, he didn't noticed the slight, dark-haired woman standing there.

She gave a little cough to attract his attention.

'Are you looking for someone?'

Even in her old clothes, she had an air about her.

'I am looking for a job – with the raspberries?'

Picking up the foreign accent, the sergeant was surprised. She didn't look like the others. For one thing, her complexion was pale, even a little sallow. She was slightly built and her hands didn't look like the hands of someone used to manual work.

She noticed his hesitation.

'I work hard, *monsieur*...'

'All right,' he said at last. 'The pails are there. Take one and away up to the last dreel on that side.'

'Dreel?'

'Row,' he explained briefly, glancing at her again. She'd not last long, this one, and the other women might make things hard for her.

Simone began picking slowly and steadily, making sure the berries were firm and clean. She enjoyed the peace and quiet as she made her way up the row, hearing occasionally the voices of the women from further up the field.

She worked quietly, lifting her head now and then to smile at one of the other pickers. From time to time, she made her way down to the weighing machine with her basket, and Jock nodded approvingly.

She might look fragile, this woman, but she was a hard worker.

'Don't be working too hard,' he chaffed her. 'There's a break quite soon.'

Simone smiled and started up the row again.

When the whistle blew there was a rush down towards the hut. The women brought out pieces, and someone started brewing up the tea.

Simone followed more slowly. How foolish she had been! She hadn't thought to bring anything but an apple and scone to eat, and she found her appetite sharpened by the fresh air.

'Have you nothing to eat?' Jeannie, one of the women, turned to her.

'An apple, and a scone.' Simone seemed embarrassed as she pronounced the Scottish word.

'We've plenty.' One of the women leaned over. 'See, here's a roll for you, and some lemonade.'

'*Merci*. You are so kind.'

The women glanced sideways at her but no-one liked to ask questions.

She sat quietly, enjoying the warmth of the sunshine and listening idly to the women's chatter. Their children played hide and seek among the rows and chased each other the length of the field.

She watched as one of the women with a baby put her child back in a battered old pram.

'You have a beautiful *bébé*, Madame,'

Simone said impulsively.

The woman's rough hand stroked the child's dark head.

'Aye, he's no' bad.' There was no mistaking the pride in her voice.

'May I...?'

The woman hesitated, then carefully handed the baby to Simone. She cradled the child in her arms, talking to him softly and rocking him backwards and forwards.

'You've bairns of your own?' the woman asked, as Simone reluctantly handed the baby back.

When Simone looked blank, she pointed to the child.

'Les enfants? Non! Pardon, Madame ... no, no children...'

The young mother put the baby back into the pram and tucked him in.

Together, the women walked up the row, and the voices died away as they began picking again, a little more slowly now in the heat of the afternoon sun.

When the day's work was finished, Simone walked back to the cottage. She wondered what Marian and Betsy would say. Should she not work in the fields? But she had enjoyed it so, feeling the warmth of the sun on her face...

Marian was sitting in the window seat of the sitting-room, a cloud of printed voile material on her lap.

She glanced up.

'My goodness, Simone! Have you been walking most of the afternoon? You've caught the sun.'

Simone smiled.

'Yes, Marian … I much like being out of the doors. I – I have been picking … *travail*, in the berryfields? You do not care too much?'

'Of course I don't mind.' Marian smiled. 'But it's hard work.'

She held up the material.

'Look, Simone – I've been busy sewing all day. I want a new dress to wear in the evening, for the party.'

'Party?'

'Paul – Mr Holt – is giving a party for the end of the berry season, up at the farm…'

Marian hesitated. She and Paul hadn't been on the best of terms, but the invitation had been a warm and welcoming one.

Simone smiled, stretching a hand out to touch the soft cloth.

'It is lovely… I like to make the clothes. It is easy for me. If you like, I could…'

'Would you really?' Marian smiled. 'Thank

150

you – *merci* – Simone.'

As Simone went upstairs, Marian looked after her. What a strange girl she was in many ways, and yet already she was very much part of the family. But would they ever get to know her really well? Sometimes, Marian had this feeling that there was a great deal more to know…

Simone was true to her word and on the day of the dance Marian whirled round while Elspeth looked at her admiringly.

'It's beautiful!'

The French girl smiled her pleasure as Marian smoothed the flower-printed voile.

'It's perfect. How clever you are, Simone. Thank you so much.'

'It is nothing.' Simone was a little embarrassed by all the praise.

Marian smiled and looked gratefully at her.

She was slowly coming to know Simone, and she was beginning to see why her brother, whom she remembered as cheerful and outgoing, and quite undemonstrative, could have chosen this woman – shy and reserved, but capable of great warmth.

As the two of them walked up the lane towards the farm that evening, they could hear the fiddle music from the barn.

'William – he loved so the *campagne* – the countryside, and the farm.' Simone shivered a little. 'Only a little time together ... but we knew ... *oui.*'

She gave a little sigh.

'Poor Simone...' Marian murmured.

Simone turned to her, eyes shining, and suddenly her face was transformed.

'I loved him, Marian,' she said, a little catch in her voice. 'So much!'

Marian was silent. How fortunate William was to have found this girl...

They were nearing the farm now, and they could hear the music and a cheerful hub-bub from the barn.

People crowded into the far end of the barn as the band struck up, nodding their approval.

The St Bernard Waltz was followed by a set of the Lancers, and Bella was up on the floor for every dance. At last, mopping her brow, she sank down on a seat beside her friend.

'Look over there.' She nudged Jeannie.

'Oh, it's the sergeant. He doesn't look as if he's enjoying himself. Well, if a body can't let their hair down on a night like this...'

'Does he never have a day off?' Bella guffawed.

'Bella!' Her friend suddenly nudged her. 'He's coming over!'

The sergeant was making his way purposefully across and stopped right in front of Bella.

'May I have the pleasure of this dance?'

Bella flushed scarlet. After all she'd said about him, here he was, asking her to dance!

Suddenly, she took pity on Sergeant Fordyce. Poor man, he didn't look the kind who ever went to a dance. And she'd bet her last tanner he was all left feet.

She glanced down at her own feet, which were surprisingly neat and dainty. He'd probably trample all over them.

'I'd be pleased to, Sergeant Fordyce,' she said.

Sarah was dancing with Paul.

'Remember how I taught you the tango and the foxtrot?'

'That old gramophone in the school room.' Paul laughed.

'Well, let's see how good a pupil you were...'

Marian was whirling by with Robert.

'I'm not much of a dancer,' he was saying apologetically.

'It doesn't matter.' Marian smiled up at him.

Jeannie, sitting at the side of the hall, kept her eyes on her friend. Poor Bella, having to dance with the sergeant... Suddenly, her eyes widened. That couldn't be them, surely? That stocky figure in the shiny blue suit who was dancing so professionally with Bella?

All the others stood back, leaving the floor to the best dancers in the hall. Bella had a natural sense of rhythm, and she responded to the sergeant's lead. As they finished with a final twirl, a round of applause broke out.

Marian cheered and clapped enthusiastically with the rest then she turned to Paul.

'He's a splendid dancer, your sergeant,' she said.

'I'd no idea.' He smiled back at her and, for a moment, she thought how pleasant it would be if they could be friends and chat normally like this, instead of always being at loggerheads.

The sergeant escorted a bemused Bella back to her seat.

'I ... I didn't know you could dance, Sergeant...'

'Fancy that!' He was clearly enjoying her discomfiture.

'Yes, well...' She was about to turn away. 'Thanks for the dance.'

'I wonder, Bella…' He paused. 'I may be able to tango, but I've never learned any reels or Strathspeys. Would you be kind enough to teach me?'

'I'll do that.' Bella beamed up at him. 'It's grand, the eightsome.'

'Then you'll save me that dance?'

She nodded.

He turned away and Jeannie giggled.

Bella rounded on her.

'He's no' that bad. Anyone who can dance like that – well, he's all right…!'

'You'll save me the last dance?'

Marian, flushed and smiling, turned to find Robert at her side.

'This is great fun, isn't it? I'm so glad Sarah persuaded Paul to open up the barn.'

How attractive she looked, Robert thought, in that silky dress, her headband low on her brow, her eyes sparkling with excitement.

'You will save me the last dance?' he asked again.

'Of course.' She smiled at him.

'Good. I'll be back.'

After the last strains of 'Auld Lang Syne' had died away, there was a cry.

'Three cheers for Mr Holt!'

Paul looked surprised, Marian thought,

but pleased, too.

'I'm glad you've enjoyed yourselves,' he called out over the babble.

'Same again next year, sir!' someone shouted, and there was a roar of approval.

Marian felt Robert's hand on her arm.

'I'll walk you down the lane when you're ready.'

She shrugged into her coat, feeling oddly flat. But why? It had been a wonderful evening. She knew she looked her best – thanks to Simone's skill with the needle. The dancing had been fun, the pickers had enjoyed it ... everyone had had a fine time. And yet ... something niggled at her.

She and Robert moved towards the door, listening to people calling goodbye to their friends.

'See you tomorrow!'

'A fine night for the walk home!'

Marian glanced up at the sky. A cloud moved over the moon and then disappeared. She shivered a little.

'Are you cold?' Robert put an arm around her.

'No, no. I'm fine.'

And then she knew just what was niggling at her. It was Simone's words from earlier. *So little time together, but we knew...*

Marian was suddenly sure that Robert would never be any more than a good friend. She could never feel for him what Simone had felt for William. But how could she hurt him?

As they walked down the lane, the shouts of the departing party guests grew fainter and the night seemed very quiet. In the shadow of an elder tree, Robert drew Marian towards him.

He put his hand under her chin and tilted her face up towards him.

'Marian, don't keep me waiting any longer. I have to know. You said you'd think it over. I wonder – have you made up your mind? Please, tell me.'

Marian hesitated. How easy it would be to say 'yes'. How it would please Betsy and the family – and what a good husband he would be. She wasn't likely to find anyone else … and yet…

'I'm sorry.' She looked up at him, a catch in her voice. 'I've thought it over and over again. I like you so much, I admire you … and…'

'But the answer's no.'

She could hardly speak.

'Robert, I'm so sorry.'

'Don't be. It's your decision.' He held her

hand between his. 'I wish it had been "yes", but I won't try to persuade you.'

They stood silently for a moment or two.

'Come on,' he said at last. 'I'll see you home. It's getting cold.'

At the door, he bent briefly and kissed her on the cheek, then turned back up the lane.

Marian watched him go, then went indoors and closed the door behind her with a heavy heart.

Chapter Six

'Simone?' Marian spoke a little sharply. What was wrong with the girl these days? Half the time her mind seemed to be elsewhere; often, you had to speak to her several times before she answered.

Marian needed some practical help with organising the afternoon's prize-giving. But instead of helping her to move books, Simone was staring dreamily out of the window.

'I am sorry.' Simone returned to the present. 'I know you have a lot to do today.'

'It's just – I do want the prize-giving to go well. Mr Lindsay's left the organising to me and I don't want anything to go wrong...'

'Tell me what I can do,' Simone said briskly, herself again.

'Would you pin up these drawings on the wall?' Marian pointed to a box of drawing-pins. 'I'll take these books along to the hall...'

An excited boy rushed into the classroom. 'You shouldn't be here, Jimmy,' Marian said sternly. 'I told you all to stay in the playground. But now you're here, you can take these books to the hall. Put them on the table. Carefully, mind! Don't rush.

'I think that's everything taken care of.' She brushed a strand of hair off her forehead. 'If only the choir remember their words ... and I hope Maisie doesn't get stagefright.'

Seeing the blank look on Simone's face, she tried to explain what the word meant and soon they were both giggling.

'You've been such a help,' Marian said, her good temper restored, 'making the costumes for the play. Everyone said how beautiful they were. I don't know how I'd have managed...'

'It's good to keep busy.' Simone smiled.

'It certainly has been a quick year.'

There flashed through Marian's mind all that had happened. How much more confident she felt now!

She remembered with a rueful smile that first day at school – the sea of unfamiliar faces looking up at her. Now, she knew every child well – and how she'd miss the older ones who were going on to secondary school.

Mr Lindsay had been complimentary

about her work – and he didn't praise lightly.

Betsy was settled and happy in the cottage, and Elspeth was doing well at the high school, practising the piano diligently up at the farmhouse.

And yet, there was something missing from her own life. It was just as well she hadn't had time to brood. Just occasionally, Marian wondered if she'd been right to turn down Robert's proposal.

He didn't call round at the cottage so often these days. Perhaps once term ended and the berry picking season began, they might be friends once more.

And Paul … hastily, she tried to put him out of her mind. She had to admit he was making a good job of running the farm. People liked him, and he was fair with his workers.

Marian had thought at one time he might become more than just a friend. But they were on friendly terms, nothing more than that.

Sometimes, he could be very pleasant and approachable, but he could also be distant.

She'd heard that he'd paid a brief visit to his family in England. That must have been Sarah's doing. Marian smiled, remembering how likeable and persuasive Paul's sister had been.

She brought herself back to the present with an effort.

Was there time for a last-minute word to the choir? Would there be enough chairs for the mothers and guests? There would be tea afterwards, and lemonade for the children.

Betsy had made scones and sponge cakes that morning.

'I think it'll be all right,' Marian murmured out loud.

'Do not worry so much,' Simone said reassuringly.

But Marian couldn't help feeling nervous. The prize-giving would no doubt go smoothly, so *why* was she anxious. Was it the thought of seeing Paul again?

This is ridiculous, Paul thought. As if he hadn't enough to do on the farm! But he'd found it hard to say no when Marian had invited him to present the prizes at the school.

He realised that he was rather looking forward to the afternoon. Was it anything to do with seeing Marian again?

Making his way to the school, he smiled at a small group of pupils hanging around the school gate.

'Hello, mister!' one of the bolder ones greeted him and, amused, Paul gave the boys a cheerful nod.

Of course, he reasoned, he'd grown to like Marian, for all her impulsive ways. But that was all. He wasn't ready for anything more, not till he'd put the war and all its horrors behind him.

Besides, he reminded himself, Marian and Robert had always seemed fairly close. An ideal match, he told himself firmly, and then wondered why he felt a little dispirited at the thought...

'Are you looking for the teacher?' A boy with a freckled face and a mop of ginger hair stood in Paul's path. 'She's in the classroom. I'll show you.'

The boy rapped on the door, then pushed it open.

'She's in here, mister!'

Paul had expected to find Marian on her own. He nodded to Simone but his gaze lingered on Marian.

'Hello, Paul.'

She greeted him pleasantly, and he thought how attractive she looked. The new pale green jumper, worn with her best skirt, was knitted in a light wool that looked like silk, and trimmed with creamy lace. The

163

colour set off her shining hair and blue eyes, and Paul realised he had never seen her look more lovely.

'I must go.' Simone excused herself after a few minutes. 'I have the – the work still to do...'

'She's been such a help,' Marian said, to cover the slight awkwardness when Simone left them alone. 'And you, too – I can't thank you enough. These are splendid prizes you've donated. It's the first time we've had one for effort.'

'Everyone needs a little encouragement,' he said, and Marian found herself blushing.

'The picnic, too,' she went on hurriedly. 'It was so good of you to pay for the treat...'

'It's nothing,' he said hastily. 'Please don't mention it – to anyone.'

What a strange man he was, Marian thought. He was so generous – look at that party he'd put on for the berry pickers. Yet he hated anyone to know of his kindness.

She hurriedly changed the subject.

'I heard you were away for a few days – down south?'

'I went home to my family in Lancashire. My father and I–'. He paused. 'Well, we hadn't been on very good terms. But Sarah's visit helped a lot. And she persuaded me to go home to try to heal the breach.'

'And did you?' Marian asked cautiously.

'I think so. It helps that the farm's doing well. My father was determined I should go into the family business, you see. But now he knows I'm making a go of this...'

'I'm glad,' Marian said warmly.

As she smiled up at him, Paul almost forgot where he was – he was aware only that there was more than just friendship between them. He had never felt like this about anyone before.

'Marian,' he began hesitantly.

'Miss, they're here!' A girl from one of the upper classes put her head round the door and the fragile moment was shattered.

'I'll take you along to Mr Lindsay's room,' Marian said, pulling herself together.

The prize-giving went just as she'd hoped. The choir sang tunefully and no-one forgot their words. The children remembered to bow as Paul handed over the prizes, and Mr Lindsay's speech was warmly applauded – especially when he praised Marian's hard work during the year.

Marian listened a little tremulously to Paul's speech, joining in the laughter at his jokes. But afterwards, she could remember very little of what he'd said.

Released from being on their best beha-
viour, the children milled around, coming
back for more cakes and buns.

The mothers chatted to Marian as if she
were an old friend and she began to relax.

'Robert! What a nice surprise! What are
you doing here?' Marian exclaimed, spot-
ting the doctor standing beside Simone at
the back of the hall.

'It's my day off.' He grinned. 'My sister
asked me along. I've a nephew who's won a
prize – for effort.'

'Young Rob.' Marian smiled. 'He's doing
very well...'

They chatted easily for a few minutes, then
Marian moved away to speak to someone
who attracted her attention.

Simone, standing silently, noted that
Robert's eyes stayed on Marian only briefly,
then he looked around the room.

'You are no longer ... sad?' she began hesitantly.

Robert turned to look at her.

'No, Simone, not any more. Marian's a
grand girl, but she was quite right to turn
me down. I admire her – greatly. But the
romance was all in my own imagination.
Friends we are and friends we'll stay, just as
it should be. One's mind can sometimes

play tricks…'

Suddenly he stopped, noticing the look of misery on Simone's face. She was obviously struggling to control her emotions.

'My dear girl…'

Simone knew she could trust him implicitly.

'Robert…?' She pronounced his name without the 't'. 'May I speak to you with the privacy, please? I would not ask, but it is very *importante*.'

Robert looked concerned.

'Well, yes, of course,' he said slowly.

'But perhaps you are busy – you have patients to see?'

He shook his head.

'This is my afternoon off. How can I help you? Do you want to come along to the surgery?'

'No, no.' Simone looked flustered as she twisted a strand of hair between her fingers. 'It is something – I cannot tell anyone, but you – I think – you, I can trust.'

Robert looked mystified.

'I'm driving my sister and nephew home. But why don't you come for a walk with me this evening and tell me what's worrying you?'

'Thank you.'

'About seven o'clock? I'll call for you.'

Robert held the gate open for Simone and, as he took her arm to help her down the steps to the path, he noticed that she was trembling. To give her time to compose herself, he strolled along, not looking at her, but chatting pleasantly about the prize-giving and the children's efforts.

'Let's take this path.' He pointed to a track that led along the burn. 'It's dry enough – it hasn't rained for a while. Oh, your shoes–' He glanced at Simone's neatly shod feet.

'They are quite all right for walking.'

Simone followed him down the path and they walked in silence.

Robert waited for her to speak, puzzled. What could be the matter? He had never, even on that first evening, known Simone to act so strangely.

'Let's sit down.' He gestured towards the trunk of a fallen tree.

Simone agreed, and they sat in silence for a moment or two, Robert waiting for her to make the first approach.

'I need to ask you...' she said at last. 'Could you give me some advice?'

'If I can,' Robert said cautiously. 'But if it's a medical problem, you really ought to come to the surgery.'

'No,' she said firmly. 'At least, it is not *my* medical problem.'

She seemed to summon up her courage.

'Doctor Robert, if someone found they had the … the tuber … how do you say it?'

'Tuberculosis?'

'Yes … what would happen to them? Could they be cured? And…'

'So that's what's worrying you!' Robert broke in. 'We can certainly have some tests done, but I'm sure you've no need to worry.

'Oh, I know you were in a pretty poor state when you arrived here, but you're strong and fit now. I'm fairly certain you've no need to be concerned…'

He broke off as Simone shook her head vigorously.

'No, no, you have misunderstood! It is not about me.'

'You must know I can't give an opinion about someone else, Simone. Can't he – or she – go to a doctor?'

She burst into tears.

'Please listen to me,' she pleaded. 'It's hard enough. I thought I could talk to you…'

'And so you can, Simone. Please, tell me the whole story. I'll listen, I promise.'

'My aunt back home, in the village, in

169

France, has the tuberculosis.' Simone dabbed at her eyes. 'I have had a letter. There is a child she looks after. Will the child be harmed? My aunt has to go away for treatment. How long before she is cured?'

'If the illness has been diagnosed – found – early, she will stand a good chance of a cure. But it's right that she should be isolated – kept away from others,' he explained.

'But the child is to be sent away!' Simone, in obvious distress, twisted her fingers together. 'To an orphanage.'

'There's no-one who could look after the child? No other relative? What about the mother? Is she dead?'

'No, she is not.' Simone gulped. 'This is what I want to tell you, Robert. It is *my* child! *I* am the mother.' She buried her face in her hands.

'Poor Simone…' Robert reached out and laid a hand on her arm. 'I had no idea – William's child.'

'It is not William's child!' Simone looked up at him defiantly. 'Please, Robert, say nothing till I've told you the whole story – perhaps then you will despise me.'

'I'll listen, I promise,' Robert said.

Simone took a deep breath.

'After William was killed, I stayed on in the

village. My mother was dead and I helped my father in the village shop. But it was difficult, and my father was seriously ill, all of that winter.

'We had so little... People had no money to buy food and sometimes I would help them – a loaf of bread, a few potatoes.' She paused.

'My father grew weaker, and we could not afford money for medicines. And then a stranger arrived in our village. He was from the south, he said, a travelling salesman.

'He made friends easily, and sometimes he would bring us little treats – wine, pâté, foods we had not seen for a long time!

'He began to court me. As if I cared for anyone but my own William! Everyone thought he was a fine young man – handsome, kind. One night, he called at our house.

'He told me he had an offer to make. If I would marry him, he would buy the shop, and we would be prosperous once again. He would run the shop and we would settle in the village.

'I refused him, of course. But he came back a few days later. "Think about it," he said. "For your family's sake..."

'Robert, I felt dead inside! I had loved

only William … now he was gone. My father was so proud of the shop … so I agreed.

'Of course,' Simone said with a catch in her throat, 'he would not wait for marriage. And what did it matter to me?' She was silent for a moment. 'What a fool I was!'

'What happened?' Robert prompted her gently.

'He went away a week or two later and I never saw or heard from him again. And then I learned I was to have a child.

'My father, my aunt – they were very angry.' She shuddered. 'I had brought shame on them. I was sent away to another aunt's home – she lived on the outskirts of Paris. And when little Pierre was born, she agreed to adopt him. I was not to visit. I was never to see him again!'

She gazed at the ground, speaking in a leaden voice.

'I write – I send money when I can, but I have never seen him since I handed him over to Tante Louise.

'Since my father died, I have had no real home – that is why I decided I must start afresh and try to find William's family. They are the first real family I have known, and they are so kind.'

'How did you find out about your aunt's

illness?' Robert asked.

'A cousin wrote to tell me. And little Pierre is to be put in an orphanage. I cannot let them do this!' she said fiercely.

'But what are you going to do?'

Robert recognised the effort she was making to tell her story. This was a new Simone, quite different from the subdued girl he had known.

'I am going back to France. What else can I do?' she said, as if there was no question about it. 'And you – you will help me, Robert, won't you?'

'If I can.' Robert hesitated. 'But, Simone, have you – I mean – do Marian and her mother know about this?'

'Oh, no!' Simone flared up. 'How could I tell them? They would be so angry. And I deserve it. No, it is better I just go away.'

'They have a right to know,' Robert said firmly. 'They've looked after you all these months. You can't just go back to France without telling them why.'

'I cannot!' Simone said vehemently. 'They would not understand. I – I have betrayed their son.'

'I think,' Robert tried to persuade her, 'that you would find they would be understanding – and sympathetic.'

Again, Simone shook her head.

'No, it is better they forget about me. But I must return to France. Pierre – he needs me. There is no-one to look after him now. Please, Robert...' she turned her gaze on him '...you will help me, won't you?'

'I'll do what I can,' he said slowly. 'But on one condition, Simone. You must tell Marian and Betsy the truth.'

'The pickers will be here again soon,' Jess declared. 'My, how the year's flown past. It seems no time since they left last year.'

Marian, rocking back and forward in the big kitchen chair, smiled.

'I'm looking forward to seeing them all again – Dougie and his family, and Bella and the others.'

'I like to see them coming off the buses,' Jess said comfortably. 'The mothers and the wee ones – all looking that pale. And when they've been here a week, you can see the change in them. The fresh air and good food – it makes a real difference.'

She began folding sheets.

'And how's your mother these days?'

'She's fine. It's done her so much good, having Simone here.' Marian paused, thinking of her sister-in-law. The girl had become

174

more and more withdrawn. Marian had been tempted to ask what was the matter, but hesitated to intrude. She decided to say nothing to Jess.

Reluctantly, she got up from the chair and stretched.

'I must be on my way. I've to go to the shops.'

'It's been fine to have a chat,' Jess began, then broke off. 'Mercy on us, what's that?'

Marian rushed to the window and Jess flung open the kitchen door.

Sergeant Neill, the local policeman, was well known in the village. He was a big man, with a cheerful, smiling face – and a comforting presence when there was trouble. But today, he looked unusually stern.

'Miss Marian!' he said. 'I was told I'd find you here. We've had a wee bit of bother.'

'Come away in.' Jess bustled at the doorway to see what was going on. Then she gasped. 'What in the name have you brought with you?'

The figure behind the policeman was grubby, covered with straw, and mud-stained, but still recognisable.

'Dougie!' Marian exclaimed at the sight of the youngster.

'He said you'd know him.' Sergeant Neill

ushered the boy into the kitchen. 'You stand there and don't try to run away…'

'What's happened?' Marian asked.

'Found him in the henhouses down at Maryfield Farm. He couldn't say why he was there – stealing, I expect.'

'I wasna!' Dougie's voice was hoarse. 'I never stole nothing.'

'He said would I talk to you and you could speak for him,' the sergeant continued.

'Where have you come from, Dougie?' Marian asked, her anxiety apparent in her sharp tone of voice. 'You're not supposed to be here till next week! Where's your mother?' She thought rapidly. 'You've run away from home…' she said at last.

Dougie, his eyes on the floor, nodded.

'I'm sure he wouldn't do anything wrong.' Marian turned to the policeman.

'I just wanted somewhere to sleep,' the boy muttered.

'He'll be hungry, poor laddie,' Jess put in.

She buttered a couple of scones and poured out a glass of milk, then set them in front of Dougie. They all watched as he wolfed down the scones and drank the milk in one long gulp. Marian wondered when he'd last eaten.

'Now,' she said, as Dougie drew a hand

across his mouth, 'tell us what happened. Your mother will be very worried about you.'

'My dad's ill,' he said in a rush. 'She's got a job in the mill but she canna leave him long. There's someone comes in and watches him and the bairn. She said we werena to go to the berries this year. She canna leave him.

'I wasna running away.' He gulped. 'I'm big enough to come on my own. I can get good money at the berries.'

'So you thought you'd help your mother by earning some money?'

He nodded, keeping his eyes on the floor.

The policeman took out his notebook.

'Give me your full name and address, lad, and we'll get a message to your mother. Then we'll see about getting you back home.'

'I wrote her a wee note,' Dougie muttered. 'I can write well enough now.' He looked sullen.

'I know you can,' Marian said encouragingly.

He looked tired, defeated and on the verge of tears. Marian could sense his despair and so could Jess.

'Wait a wee bit. It's true he could earn good money at the berries. And it'd help his mother,' Jess said.

'Maybe,' the policeman said. 'But who's going to look after him? He's too young to stay in the bothy with the men.'

'He can stay with us!' Jess offered suddenly. 'Bob'll not object and I'll not mind having a lad to cook for.'

'Would you, Jess?' Marian could have hugged her.

'As long as your mother agrees. And you'll have to behave yourself, mind,' Jess warned the boy.

'Oh, aye!' Dougie beamed. 'And I'll work real hard.'

'Then that's settled,' Jess said cheerfully. 'Now, son, could you manage another scone?'

During the weeks that followed, Marian kept an eye on Dougie. She was pleased to find that the boy was settling in well. His mother, once she had recovered from her alarm over his disappearance, was glad he was to spend the summer in the country.

He's a good boy, really, she wrote to Marian, *but it's hard with his father being ill.*

By now, Marian knew most of the pickers as old friends, and she was amused to find how readily they accepted Sergeant Fordyce. This year he was easier with them, and accepted their teasing with good humour.

Geordie and Bob seemed happy to leave the supervision of the pickers to the sergeant.

Marian met Geordie one day on her way back from the village. He was leaning against a gate, standing very still.

'Hello,' she called out cheerfully. 'Having a break?'

Immediately, Marian regretted her words, noticing how much older and weaker Geordie looked. When he walked across to meet her, he moved with some difficulty.

'Are you all right?' she asked anxiously.

'Just a touch of rheumatics,' he replied with a grim smile.

'But...' Marian was about to say that the weather was unusually dry. Then she paused. Why hadn't she noticed that he was getting older, and finding it hard to keep up with the younger men?

'I'll need to think about retiring soon,' he said. 'But I'd miss this place.'

Marian's thoughts were heavy when she went home. The farm without Geordie? It was unthinkable. But perhaps it *was* time he retired. He'd have more hours to spend in the trim garden he'd made at his cottage.

How proud he was of the chrysanthemums he grew every year, and the prizes he won at the local show...

By now, the pickers were working from early morning, taking advantage of the fine weather. Marian sometimes went up to the fields, taking a batch of biscuits for their tea-break.

One especially hot afternoon, when there was no breath of wind over the fields, she came across Bella sitting by the end of a dreel, her legs stretched out and a handkerchief over her face.

She looked up with a start.

'Och, it's just you, miss,' she said when she saw Marian. 'I thought it was the gaffer.'

'Sergeant Fordyce?' Marian smiled.

Bella nodded.

'Mind you, him and me are good pals now. He'd not mind me having a wee break.'

'It's hard work in this heat,' Marian sympathised.

'Och, he's not that bad.' Bella paused. 'Him and me – we're going to the pictures on Saturday night.'

'Oh.' Marian didn't quite know what to say. 'I hope you have a nice time, then, Bella.'

'I will that.' She heaved herself to her feet. 'I'd better get back. Mind you, he's fair,

Sergeant Fordyce – treats everyone the same.

'I'm pleased he's to be getting out of that bothy. Geordie's cottage'll do him fine, now that he's retiring.' She nodded to Marian and made her way up the dreel.

Marian stood still, trying to make sense of what she had just heard.

Geordie retiring? Well, she'd known that wasn't far off. But to be put out of the little cottage that had been his home? With no wife to take care of him, Geordie had learned early in life to cook and mend and keep a house clean.

His home was shining, with floors spotless and brasses gleaming.

And now, what was to happen to him? How could Paul be so heartless? To turn away a loyal worker like that, just because he wanted the cottage for the sergeant... What a cruel thing to do!

On her way home, Marian was seething inside. This mustn't happen... She wouldn't let it happen!

Marian stormed into the cottage, where her mother was sitting in the window-seat, darning Elspeth's stockings.

'Is there something wrong?' Betsy asked.

'There certainly is!'

Underneath Marian's anger, there was disappointment. She had thought she knew Paul. She'd come to see him as caring, and considerate of other people's feelings. How wrong she had been!

'Well?' Betsy prompted. 'Aren't you going to tell me?'

'It's so unfair...' Marian launched into the story Bella had told her. 'Geordie's been so loyal all these years – and now, to be turned out like this. It's appalling!'

'It may not be true, dear,' Betsy suggested mildly.

'Why not? It's just the sort of thing he would do!' Marian's voice rose.

'I'm afraid,' Betsy said slowly, 'that if it's all arranged, there isn't a great deal we can do...'

'Oh, yes, there is! I'm going up to the farm to see Paul Holt – now. He can't get away with treating people like this, Mother.'

'Be careful,' Betsy warned her. 'Don't go saying something you'll regret...'

Marian was so impulsive! Betsy sighed. Even as a child, she'd had a strong sense of justice, which often landed her in trouble. But there, she thought, looking at her daughter's flushed face and firm mouth,

Marian was a grown woman now.

'I won't be long,' Marian promised. 'What I've got to say will only take a few minutes...'

She swung round as they heard the wheels of a car crunching over the gravel.

'Visitors – and just now!' Marian said impatiently. 'Oh, it's Robert,' she added.

'That's nice – we haven't seen him for some time.' Betsy rose and put away her work.

'Simone's with him,' Marian said. 'He must have given her a lift back from the village.'

Betsy opened the door.

'Come in, both of you. I'll just put the kettle on. My, Robert, you're quite a stranger these days.'

Marian noticed, with a sudden sinking of her heart, that their expressions were solemn. In fact, Simone looked almost afraid. What was the matter?

Robert put an arm round Betsy.

'Don't put the kettle on yet,' he told her gently. 'Please – won't you sit down? Marian, too.'

'What's all this about?' Marian tried to be lighthearted and off-hand. 'Dear me, you both look so serious.'

Robert glanced from one to the other.
'Simone has something she wants to tell you, something you ought to know. Go ahead, Simone...'

Chapter Seven

'Simone has something to tell you...' Robert's tone was serious and Betsy looked up inquiringly.

'Go ahead, Simone,' he urged gently, stepping back to let the girl forward.

'I'm sorry,' Marian interrupted. 'Your news will have to keep for now. I have something very important to do!'

She flung on her jacket, brushing past Robert and Simone as she ran out of the door.

'But...' Simone began.

Marian didn't hear her. She was already hurrying up the lane.

Would she be too late? Was Paul the kind of man who would change his mind about Geordie's home if she appealed to him? She felt angry and disappointed. He'd seemed so fair-minded and straightforward. But if he could do this to Geordie... She hurried on, her hands in her pockets.

Usually, she enjoyed the walk – she liked looking out for wild flowers in the hedgerows, or stopping to listen to a lark singing high in the sky. But today, she had no time for anything except her rage against Paul.

'Well, isn't this nice...'

Jess paused in putting a dish into the oven, and she turned to smile at Marian.

'I've come to see Paul.'

'Oh, it's early yet.' Jess glanced at the clock. 'He'll not be in for a while. Won't you sit down and have a cup of tea, Miss Marian? I've pancakes, freshly made.'

'No thanks, Jess.' Marian was deflated, but only for a moment. 'I'll walk down to the fields and find him.'

'Dear me, can't it wait?' Jess smiled. 'It's surely very important!'

Marian Meldrum hadn't changed much since she was about Elspeth's age, Jess thought fondly... Always dashing about, full of some ploy or new enthusiasm, quick to stand up for anyone she thought was being unfairly treated.

'It *is* important, Jess.'

The older woman glanced out of the window.

'You're in luck, then. I can see him coming into the yard now. He must have finished early.'

Paul paused in the doorway.

186

'I'm going into town, Jess,' he began, then stopped when he saw Marian.

'Hello!' he greeted her cheerfully. 'It's good to see you, Marian...' His voice trailed off. 'Is there something wrong?'

'I need to talk to you,' she said, trying to keep her voice even.

'Goodness.' Paul looked a little puzzled, but then he grinned. 'My errand will have to wait, then. Come into my study. Would you like a cup of tea?'

'No, thank you,' Marian said briskly. 'What I've got to say won't take long.'

Paul flung himself into the chair and mopped his forehead.

'Whew! We're in for a storm, I reckon.'

Marian remained standing by the door.

'Come on, Marian,' he said, a little impatiently. 'Do sit down. If you continue to stand there, I'll have to do the gentlemanly thing and get up, and I'd like a few minutes to have a bit of a rest...'

A little grudgingly, she took a chair opposite him.

'Now then...' He smiled. 'What's so vitally important?'

'It's Geordie,' she burst out. 'How *could* you do such a thing? I thought you were a decent and fair man, but you're nothing of the kind! You come up here with your ruthless way of running things. Well, you can't treat people like that!'

Her face flushed, she paused for breath.

'Marian ... what have I done now?' Paul was exasperated. 'You rush in here, accusing me of being a – a tyrant. Stop ranting like a fishwife and calm down.'

'Don't you call me a fishwife!' Marian glared at him. 'You know perfectly well what you've done! Geordie's been with us for nearly forty years, and he's lived happily all that time in his little cottage. And the garden – that's his pride and joy.

'But as soon as he's not able to work, he's being put out, just like that! Where is he supposed to go? The workhouse? Or hadn't you even thought about that?'

Paul rose and pulled Marian to her feet, holding her firmly by the elbow.

'Now listen to me! No!' he insisted, as she tried to speak. 'It's my turn now. You seem to have got hold of quite the wrong end of this stick. *No-one's* putting Geordie out of his cottage! He's retiring because he's not able to cope with the work any more.'

'So why are you turning him out?' she demanded.

Paul put his fingers over her lips.

'Listen, please! Geordie *is* retiring, but he wants to go. And he isn't being forced out of the cottage...'

Marian tried to struggle out of his grasp.

'So why is Sergeant Fordyce going into Geordie's house?'

'Will you calm down, please?' Paul's voice rose. 'It's Geordie's choice. He's moving to Inverness because his sister's been recently widowed. They're going to share a house, with a garden big enough for his roses, he tells me.'

'Oh...' Marian was deflated. 'I didn't know.'

'No, you didn't, did you?' Paul looked down at her.

Marian felt a pang of remorse, then sadness. At one time, she would have known all that was happening in her employees' lives, but now...

It was perfectly reasonable when you thought about it. She'd often heard Geordie speak about his sister, Mary. They'd be content, sharing a home. Of course, that was the best solution for everyone...

She felt herself blushing. What a fool Paul must think her. Storming in here and ranting like – well, a fishwife. Hadn't he just said so?

'Paul, I'm so sorry,' she said slowly. 'I didn't mean to fly off the handle. It was just that I was anxious about Geordie. He's been a good friend to our family...'

He was smiling now, to her relief.

'I should be used to your impulsive ways by now, shouldn't I? If I had sixpence for every time you've flown off the handle...'

'I don't, often,' Marian interrupted. 'Do I?'

'All the time,' he said solemnly, still smiling.

'Now you're teasing me,' she said softly.

'But isn't it worth it, for the making up afterwards?' he asked. 'And this time, I think we should make up properly.'

His arms went round her as he found her lips in a long, lingering kiss.

'There,' he said at last, 'I've wanted to do that for a long time.'

'Mr Holt!' Jess's voice called from the hall. 'You're wanted on the telephone!'

Paul turned back to Marian.

'I've lots more to tell you. Promise you'll come back this evening?'

'I promise.' Marian's mind was in a whirl, and she felt dizzy. She had never felt like this before; certainly not with Robert. She couldn't really be in love with Paul ... could she?

How different everything seemed now! Marian felt light-headed as she made her way down the lane. She could hardly believe it – Paul Holt, who had seemed so aloof, had actually kissed her!

She'd thought at one time they could be friends, but that was all. She'd even promised his sister, Sarah, that she would look out for someone suitable for him! Marian almost skipped along the path with happiness.

And tonight, she'd be seeing him again...

She had quite forgotten Robert and Simone, who had something to tell them – something important. What could it possibly be?

She pushed open the door.

'Mother! Simone! I'm back...' she began, then stopped.

Betsy was sitting in the rocking chair by the hearth. She glanced up when she saw Marian, hastily slipping her handkerchief up her sleeve.

'Mother... What's wrong? Where's Simone?'

'She's upstairs packing,' Betsy said tonelessley. 'I'm not having her spending another night in this house!'

'But what's happened? Where's Robert?'

'He's got work to do.' Betsy rose. 'And so

have I.' She smoothed down her apron and picked up a tea towel.

'Mother!' Marian caught at Betsy's hand. 'Won't you sit down and tell me what's the matter?'

'I've been made a fool of, that's all,' Betsy said sharply. 'And so have you, and–' her voice broke '–and so has William's memory.'

'I can't understand what you mean until you tell me. Mother?' Marian was bewildered.

Betsy's fingers traced the ridges along the worn wooden draining-board. Still she said nothing.

Gently, Marian put her arm round her mother's shoulder.

'Tell me, please.'

'Simone ... I can hardly bear to speak of her,' she whispered, her voice trembling. 'She's got a bairn – by another man. Since William...' She broke off.

'What ... what did she tell you?'

'Just that.' Betsy mopped her eyes. 'When I think of the months we've cared for her. If I'd known, I'd never have let her over the door!'

Marian drew a deep breath.

'But we mustn't be too harsh. There may be a good reason for...'

'Reason!' Betsy spoke sharply. 'There's no *reason* – she's betrayed my son, that's what she's done.'

'I need to hear the whole story from Simone,' Marian said gently. 'She's upstairs, you said?'

'Packing, and good riddance, too...' Betsy sniffed.

'What's the matter? Have I missed something?' Elspeth stood framed in the doorway, swinging her tennis racquet, looking from her mother to Marian.

Betsy looked up, her face a picture of misery.

'She's old enough to know.'

Marian glanced at her sister. 'I'll tell you later. I must go and see Simone.'

She knocked on the door.

'May I come in?'

Simone whirled round.

'Ah, it is you, Marian.'

She turned back to folding clothes, placing them carefully into her battered suitcase.

'Please, Simone,' Marian said gently, 'won't you stop that and tell me what has happened? I wish you'd spoken to me first, instead of Mother.'

Simone's face was empty of any expression.

'She is hurt and angry, I know, but...'
Suddenly, she burst into tears. 'Marian,
don't you understand? I could not keep it to
myself any longer! You have all been so good
to me...'

'Tell me...' Marian sat down on the bed
and put her arm around Simone's shoulders.

The girl gulped and began the story.

When she had finished there was silence
between them for a little.

'I understand ... I think,' Marian said
slowly. 'I know how desperate you must have
been. How you wanted to help your father...
And if it meant marriage to someone you
didn't love then that was brave of you.'

'I have only ever loved one man.' Simone
lifted her chin. 'And that was William.'

'I know.' Marian reached out for Simone's
hand. 'But now you must think of your son.
He's your child and he needs you. You must
go to him – right away.'

She jumped to her feet and began to fold
one of Simone's blouses.

'I'll help you all I can. And there will
always be a home for you here, I promise.'

Simone shook her head.

'Your mother will never forgive me.'

'Of course she will.' Marian spoke with

more optimism than she felt. 'She just needs time. Now,' she said briskly, 'let's pack up your things and I'll find out about the times of the trains. It's a long journey so the sooner you set out the better.'

When Marian went downstairs she found Betsy grimly preparing the tea, and Elspeth laying the table.

'Well?' Betsy turned to her elder daughter. 'And what has she got to say for herself? She'd get round you, I expect.'

'It's not like that,' Marian retorted. 'She'll be leaving as soon as possible. I'll go with her to the station...'

'Just as I said,' Betsy sniffed. 'Well, she needn't expect *me* to forgive and forget ... I won't.'

'Nor will I.' Elspeth jumped up. 'I agree with Mother. I won't forgive her, either! And to think I gave up my room to her...'

'Be quiet, Elspeth,' Marian said sharply. Her sister sniffed and went on laying the table, banging down the knives and forks.

Silently, Marian watched her mother going to and fro, her lips set in a firm line. There was no point in trying to persuade Betsy to change her mind. Perhaps, in due course, she might think more kindly of Simone.

But that would be a long time ahead.

Early the next morning, Marian went with Simone to the station at Coupar Angus. There was nothing more to be said. Simone's face was white and there were dark shadows under her eyes.

Marian knew that the girl hadn't slept. She herself had lain awake for some hours before she fell into a troubled sleep.

They waited on the platform for the train. At this time of morning there were few travellers. A light breeze stirred the branches of the beech trees, and a blackbird chirped insistently from the top of a telegraph pole.

'How beautiful it all is, and how peaceful ... I shall miss you all, so much,' Simone said suddenly. 'Doctor Robert has been so kind, too. I have promised to return the money he has loaned me ... I will send it back to him, once I have found work...'

Marian turned to her.

'You will come back, Simone, won't you?'

The girl shook her head.

'I don't know...'

Marian said nothing more. When the train drew in, she helped Simone aboard with her suitcase, and gave her a warm hug.

'Remember, you always have a home

here,' she told the girl.

And then the train was gone, taking Simone with it. Marian turned away. Despite her brave words, she was afraid – for Simone, for Betsy, and for the unknown child.

'Dougie!' Jess called. 'Come away back. You've forgotten your piece.'

'Are you that keen to get to your work? You'd have been hungry by piece time.' She handed him the neatly wrapped package. 'They're your favourite, cheese and pickle.'

Dougie beamed.

'Thanks, Jess.' He peeped into the packet.

'Away you go and don't be eating them before you get there!'

She smiled as the boy set off across the yard, whistling cheerfully. My, but he looked a different lad already, she thought. The fresh air was agreeing with him and he'd lost his pale, pinched look.

She turned back to her chores. The boy was no bother, and good company, too. Bob enjoyed teaching him skills, and he was quick to learn. The night before, he'd watched Bob whittling a piece of wood into the shape of a boat, and wanted to try it himself.

He'd been sharp, too, learning to play

dominoes, and was triumphant when he managed to win a game.

And then a thought struck Jess. It would be possible, wouldn't it? All day, as she prepared the dinner and folded the clothes to be ironed, and swept the yard and fed the hens, the thought kept coming back.

She would talk to Bob tonight, after the lad had gone to bed.

Later, as she sat darning one of Dougie's jerseys, she glanced at Bob. She knew how much her man missed their own lad who was far away in British Columbia.

'Bob,' she said suddenly, 'why don't we keep him?'

'Keep who?' Bob was filling his pipe and not paying much attention.

'Dougie.' It all came out in a rush. Couldn't the boy stay with them after the berry picking was over? He could go to the village school. After all, Miss Marian had helped him all last summer with his reading.

What chance would a lad like him have at home, with his father ill and his mother worn out with the other bairns? He might get into bother, he was too high spirited.

If he stayed, he would get a good grounding in farming. He'd be fourteen in a couple of years and leaving school. And, then, surely Mr Holt would find a job for him on the farm?

He'd be a real good worker – Dougie was made for the country life. It broke her heart to think of the boy going into the jute mills...

'I see you've thought it all out, lass.' Bob smiled.

'Well, it's a good idea, isn't it?' Jess asked eagerly.

'Aye. But I'll need to think it over,' her husband said slowly. 'And of course, his mother might not be willing. But I'd not like to see that boy cooped up in a mill, either.

'We'll sleep on it.' He picked up the newspaper. 'And in the meantime, say nothing to Dougie.'

Next day, Jess went down to the cottage to talk to Marian. She'd hesitated before going. Everyone knew there had been some sort of upset over Simone – the girl had left quickly, and no-one liked to ask when she was coming back.

Although Jess and Betsy were good friends, Jess was reluctant to raise the subject. But her heart went out to her friend, who sat listlessly in the rocking chair, a piece of knitting lying in her lap.

'I've come to ask Marian's advice,' she

began. 'About young Dougie.'

'I hope he's not being a trouble to you.'

'Not him!' Jess laughed. 'He's a pleasure to have around. No, we thought, Bob and I, he could maybe stay on with us and get his schooling here.'

'That's a very good idea, Jess.' Marian stood in the doorway, her hands full of the roses she'd just picked. 'Let me put these in water and I'll sit down and hear all about it.'

Jess explained her idea.

'But, of course, we've said nothing yet to Dougie,' she added.

'I could write to his mother, if you like,' Marian put in thoughtfully. 'I know she was glad that Dougie was to stay on for the summer.

'And I could talk to Paul – Mr Holt, that is.'

It gave her a little dart of joy to say his name. Since that astonishing kiss just a week ago, she'd hardly seen him, but she knew he'd be working long hours on the farm.

'I'll write to Dougie's mother today,' Marian promised.

It wasn't till after church on Sunday that she caught a glimpse of Paul as she was about to set off down the path.

'Do you mind if I walk back with you?' He smiled at her. 'We've seen nothing of each other lately.'

They chatted easily about the farm, and then Marian broached the subject of Dougie.

'He's a good worker for his age,' Paul agreed. 'And he's no trouble at all, so Jock tells me. The boy deserves a chance.

'I'll see that Bob and Jess aren't dipping into their own pockets for him. He'll need boots for the winter, and warm clothes ... I'll gladly pay for anything he needs.'

Marian looked up at him and wondered how she could ever have thought him uncaring and distant.

'I meant to ask you,' he went on, 'about Simone.'

She drew a deep breath and told him the whole story. He listened, not asking questions, but nodding from time to time.

'Poor Simone,' he said when he added hastily, 'no-one knows, outside the family. Except Robert.'

He turned to her suddenly, grasping her hands between his.

'Marian,' he said urgently, 'I have to know about you and Robert... Is there anything between you?'

'No, not now.' Marian smiled and shook her head. 'There never really was. We were just friends from a long time ago. He was a great help when I was lonely and rather unhappy...'

'And now?' He paused. 'You're not unhappy any more?'

'No, Paul, not any more...'

'You mean I'm getting to stay here?' Dougie looked at Jess in astonishment.

'You'll need to behave yourself, mind, and not get up to any mischief,' Jess warned him.

Dougie was a little bemused.

'But what'll my mither say?'

'She's agreed,' Marian reassured him. 'And I'll take you to Dundee once a month so that you can see your parents.'

'And I'll go to the school here?'

Marian nodded.

'And maybe get to work on the farm?'

'Would you like that?' Marian smiled.

'Would I!' Dougie gave a shout of joy, and rushed out into the yard, where Jess and Marian could see him turning cartwheels to give vent to his feelings.

Marian turned to Jess.

'I think we can say Dougie's happy about

the arrangement!'

On the way home, Marian indeed felt happier than she had done for some time. Dougie's future looked bright. And she remembered how the sergeant and Bella had looked abashed when she met them strolling along the road, Bella's hand tucked into the crook of Jock's arm.

She'd greeted them cheerfully, and made some comment about it being a fine evening.

Bella had seized on this.

'Aye. Sergeant Fordyce and me ... we thought it was too grand an evening to stop in.'

Jock hadn't looked at all embarrassed, then, and had held firmly on to Bella's hand.

Was it a romance? Well, what could be more suitable, Marian thought. The sergeant would make a fine husband, and Bella, for all her outspoken ways, had a warm, generous heart.

Marian chided herself for her matchmaking and wrenched her thoughts back to the present. Betsy still hadn't forgiven Simone, and Marian thought it best to leave the matter alone.

But often, during the past week, she had caught her mother sighing, and wondered if she was missing Simone.

Marian allowed her mind to drift, as if she had been saving some particularly happy thoughts for last. She realised that she was thinking of Paul most of the time, and the sight of his tall figure and the sound of his voice made her heart beat faster.

Quite ridiculous, she told herself. Only a short time ago we were quarrelling whenever we met! How quickly her feelings had changed...

As she pushed open the door of the cottage, Marian came down to earth again. Her mother was putting dishes away in the big cupboard where she displayed her favourite pieces – a pretty jug hand-painted with irises, a mug inscribed with the word *A Present from Largs,* and a dainty rosebud-sprigged cup and saucer.

Marian noticed with a sudden pang that her mother was moving more slowly, almost like an old woman. She had never thought of Betsy as growing older – her mother's energy had always been legendary.

She was up by half-past six every morning, and seemed tireless. Her days were spent cleaning, baking, calling on old friends and helping anyone who was in trouble. Betsy ageing? It was impossible.

'Won't you sit down for a bit? I could do that for you.' Marian offered.

Betsy shook her head.

'I like to be occupied.'

'You look tired. Simone isn't around to help out now.'

Betsy turned round.

'You'll please me by not mentioning that name in my house...'

'Mother,' Marian chided, 'if you'd only listen. You haven't really heard her side of the story. I'm sure you wouldn't feel this way if you could try to understand how hard it must have been for her.

'Simone was promised to this man to try to help her family – there was no thought of being disloyal to William...'

Betsy was implacable.

'She should never have come here.'

Marian realised there was no point in trying to talk Betsy round. Maybe, later on, her mother would feel differently. But not now...

It was one of those days in late summer meant for sitting in the sun, shelling peas, sewing, or just idling, as Marian was doing now.

She sat on the seat in front of the cottage, enjoying the sunshine and watching the grey cat busily licking its paws in the shade of a rose bush.

Everything was going to be all right, she was sure. One day, Simone and Betsy would be reconciled, as Paul and his father had been. Elspeth would have the chance to study music. Bella and her sergeant would live happily ever after.

And Paul ... with every passing day, she and Paul were growing closer.

'After the harvest,' he'd promised, 'we'll have a day out, away from the farm. We'll have lunch, see a matinée in Edinburgh – whatever you like...'

It was hard to believe that it was only two years since he'd first arrived in Blairgowrie. Now it seemed to Marian that he'd been part of her life for much longer.

And there was so much to look forward to! School would begin again soon, and Marian had lots of plans. She wanted the children to learn about their own village and the countryside.

Maybe they'd do a project on local history – it would make a good exhibition, she thought, and they could invite their parents to see all their hard work.

And Dougie would be one of her pupils this year. Marian smiled, thinking of this bright young lad and his endless curiosity.

The sound of the gate opening made her sit up suddenly. It seemed meant, somehow, that she had just been dreaming about Paul, and now, here he was.

'This is a surprise.' She smiled. 'Come in!'

It was then she noticed how white and strained he looked. He didn't answer her greeting.

'I wanted to see you again before ... before I go,' he began.

'Where are you going?'

Marian felt suddenly chilled.

'It's bad news, I'm afraid.' He paused. 'I had a telegram from Sarah. It's my father. He died suddenly in the night!'

'Oh, Paul. I'm so sorry! What a shock for you. And for your mother, and Sarah.'

'Mother will take it hard.' Paul nodded. 'I'm needed there, of course, to make the arrangements. And to see to the business. Father hasn't been well enough to do much for a long time, it seems.'

He was silent for a moment.

'I'm going south on the train tonight, Marian. I've just come to say goodbye.'

'At least it must be a little comfort, to know that you went to see your father just lately.'

'Yes, that is a comfort,' Paul agreed. 'We were never very close, but I'm glad there was no bad feeling between us any more.'

He put a hand on Marian's arm.

'Will you say goodbye to your mother and Elspeth for me, my dearest?'

'Of course I will,' she said softly, feeling tears close.

'I must go.' He hesitated, then took a few steps away from her.

'Paul?' She wanted to say so many things ... to be reassured that he wouldn't have to leave the farm.

But she knew it wasn't the right time to ask these questions. More than anything, she wanted him to kiss her goodbye.

'I'll help in any way I can,' she said quickly.

'Thank you, Marian.' He held her gaze for a moment. 'That's very kind of you.'

And then, with a wave, he was gone.

Marian sank down on the seat. Suddenly, it seemed as if the peace and contentment of the late summer afternoon had been shattered into fragments. She sat for a few moments, trying to take in his words.

She felt for Paul, and his mother, and Sarah, that cheerful, friendly girl who'd come into village life like a gust of clean, fresh air.

Then she rose and made her way slowly indoors. She knew that things would change now. Would Paul have to take over the business? Would this mean the end of his new life on the farm? And would he disappear from her life, perhaps for ever?

Chapter Eight

Marian couldn't help smiling. Suddenly, she seemed to be more aware of everything around her – the shrill voices of the children playing peevers in the playground, the beech trees along the lane, their leaves slowly turning to gold, the first frost sparkling on the grass in the early morning.

It was only a matter of time, she thought, before Paul came back. And then...

She was sad for him, of course – and for his mother and Sarah.

Even though Paul and his father had never been close, Laurence Holt's death had come as a shock. And it meant that, without warning, Paul had had to take charge of the family business. She could well imagine how he would set about things – capably, conscientiously, determined to do his best for the family.

Sitting upstairs in her room, Marian tried to compose the right sort of letter to him. It would be friendly and sympathetic, and not make any demands on him. She looked out over the garden, at the last brilliant red dahlias and a few fading roses, and thought about Paul.

How she missed him! It wasn't the same without the chance of a meeting in the lane, without his visits to the school... She sighed, and blotted the page she had written.

For the next week, Marian looked out for old Sandy the postman coming up the lane with a reply.

'Anything for me?' she would ask carelessly.

At long last, there was news. But hardly a letter Marian thought, feeling somewhat hurt and disappointed. It was more of a brief note.

Paul thanked her and her mother for their sympathy. Yes, he was busy – there was a lot to be sorted out. There was no word of when he was returning, only a brief thank you for her offer of help with the business side of the farm. His accountant would see to all that...

Marian, looking at the strong, sloping handwriting, tried to read more into his note. He ended with the words, *kind regards to you all.* No love, no warmth, no longing...

One evening, as she sat upstairs marking

some of the children's work, Marian heard a sudden noise downstairs. Then there were footsteps on the gravel, the sound of the door opening, and voices. She heard Betsy's reply, surprised, but welcoming.

Marian hurriedly brushed her hair and smoothed down her skirt, noticing the ink stains on her fingers, then went downstairs to meet the visitor. It couldn't be ... could it?

With a sudden, unreasoning hope, Marian paused on the threshold of the kitchen.

'You'll not mind us calling unexpectedly?' Sergeant Fordyce said.

'I told him, maybe it wasn't suitable.' Bella appeared behind Jock.

'Only we've a bit of news,' she went on quickly, 'and we want you both to know about it, Mrs Meldrum.'

Betsy paused, the kettle in her hand.

'Please sit down,' Marian invited.

'I'd sooner stand, miss.'

The sergeant looked suddenly abashed.

'Oh, you! I'll do the telling,' Bella interrupted him. 'The fact is, Jock and me ... well, we're going to be married.'

'I might have guessed.' Marian smiled, immediately going forward to shake hands with the sergeant.

'Well, we must celebrate! It's lovely news, my dear.' Betsy put an arm round Bella. 'I hope you'll both be very happy.'

'Thank you kindly.' Bella beamed at Jock. 'I'll look after him well. And it's a fine wee cottage...'

'So, when's the wedding to be?' Marian asked.

'We see no sense in waiting,' the sergeant said. 'It'll be as soon as the banns are called. We've been to see the minister, and he'll marry us.'

'Miss...' Bella turned shyly to Marian. 'Geordie's going to stand witness for Jock, and I was wondering if you would do the same for me?'

Marian felt a lump in her throat and she swallowed quickly.

'Of course, Bella. I'd be honoured.' She looked at the rosy face beaming with contentment and happiness.

'We've mentioned it to Jess,' the sergeant continued, 'and she's kindly offered to let us have the wedding breakfast up at the farm. Just a few friends – like yourselves.' He turned to face Betsy. 'She said she was sure Mr Holt wouldn't mind.'

'No,' Marian said quickly. 'I'm sure he wouldn't mind at all.'

'It's a sad business about his father.' Bella sighed. 'Will he be coming back here, do you know, miss? Or will he have to run the family business now?'

'I've really no idea,' Marian said evenly. 'We must wait and see, I suppose.'

Although the next few weeks were all hustle and bustle, Marian had time to notice that Betsy was quieter than usual. She was bright enough when people called in at the cottage, but now and then she would just sit, her hands folded in her lap.

That wasn't like her mother, Marian thought. Usually, she was never still, and when she did sit down, she always had a piece of mending in her hands, or a stocking to knit.

'I'm fine,' she'd answer briskly when Marian asked. 'Quite all right, dear. Don't fret, please.'

But still Marian worried that her mother seemed pale and a little drawn. She had hardly any appetite. Although she continued to make her usual appetising meals, her own helping was often left untouched.

Marian said nothing but, meeting Robert in the village one day, she told him of her concern.

'There's something wrong, Robert. I don't

know what it is, and she won't say. I don't suppose…? I'm really asking you as a friend, not a doctor. Could you possibly find out what's troubling her?'

'Of course,' Robert said warmly. 'I'll drop by and have a chat with her.'

He put a hand on Marian's shoulder and looked down into the anxious blue eyes.

'Don't worry, Marian. I'm sure she'll be fine.'

Robert made sure that Marian would still be at school when he called the next day. There was no sign of Elspeth either, so he'd be able to talk to Betsy alone.

'My, this is a surprise!' She greeted him warmly. 'You've time for a cup of tea, Robert?'

'There's always time for a cup of tea – if you'll join me?'

He waited till the tea had been poured and Betsy had pressed him to accept a slice of fruit cake.

'I thought I'd just drop in to see how you were getting on,' he began.

'Oh, you did, did you?' Betsy's shrewd gaze was fixed on the young man. 'I wouldn't be a bit surprised if that daughter of mine had asked you to call in. She'd no right.' She sounded cross.

'There's no deceiving you, is there?' Robert smiled.

'You've a good daughter in Marian, and yes, she did mention that you were looking a bit under the weather.'

He leaned across the table.

'Not eating – not sleeping, either?'

'I'm fine, really.' Betsy paused.

'Then what's troubling you?' he said gently. 'You can tell me, you know. I'm your friend as well as your doctor.'

'It's Simone,' Betsy said, wiping her eyes. 'You know the whole story, don't you? About the man who promised to buy the shop and marry her, then left her with a bairn.

'I felt she'd been deceitful and I told her to go and not come back.

'But I miss the girl – we got on well together.' She reached for her handkerchief. 'Robert ... I don't know if I can ever forgive her. And that makes me feel so sad.' She looked beseechingly at him.

'If I took her back, it wouldn't be the same. How could it? But I know Marian thinks I'm being hard.'

Robert said nothing.

'You see,' she went on, 'it's the child. I doubt if I could ever accept the child. If

216

things had been different–' her voice was low and Robert could hardly hear what she said '–it might have been William's bairn. My own grandson. But it's not – and you can't change things, can you?'

Robert stretched a hand across the table. After a moment, Betsy gripped it, and her eyes filled with tears.

Many miles away, Paul was pacing the floor. He knew he would have to let his mother and sister know of his dilemma. He couldn't put it off any longer. He'd tell them after dinner that evening...

'Let's have some music!' Sarah cheerfully set down her coffee cup after they'd finished their meal. 'Mother, what would you like to listen to?'

She sat down beside the gramophone and started thumbing through the pile of records.

'Wait!' At the insistent tone of Paul's voice, Sarah turned towards her brother.

'I've got something to tell you – and Mother.

'There's no easy way to say this,' he went on, trying to break the news gently. 'I'm afraid the firm is doing very badly. With one thing and another, first the war, then the

Depression... We're in serious trouble.'

Sarah looked up at him.

'But that's surely a temporary setback? Lots of businesses are finding it hard. My friend Bertie's father–'

Paul shook his head.

'I'm afraid it's much worse than that, Sarah. Unless things improve a great deal – we're going to have to sell.'

'Oh, Paul, you can't mean it!' Grace Holt fingered the locket which held the picture of her late husband.

Now Paul understood how Marian must have felt when she'd been told the same news by the family solicitor two years ago. A farm run down and no money left to invest.

How she must have hated my turning up and buying her old home, he thought.

He kept thinking about her, the way she'd looked when she said goodbye to him. The way she would brush a lock of hair out of her eyes...

Paul started trying to explain the financial situation to them – his efforts to keep the firm afloat, and the discussions with the bank.

There were only two choices, he'd realised. He could sell his farm and put the money into the business. But that would mean giving up all his hopes. And things were going so well now.

How he hated the factory – the noise, the dirt, the sheer monotony of it all. But if it meant saving the family business, didn't his duty lie there?

Or he could return to the farm, go his own way, forget about trying to save the business and follow his heart.

And abandon everything your father had worked for, a small insistent voice inside him said.

The weeks passed. Conscientiously, Paul went to the factory every day and held long discussions with the foreman. Together, they tried to find ways to improve production.

'It'll take a while,' the foreman warned him, speaking frankly.

Paul knew that. His father had seemed to lose heart when Paul had turned his back on the factory and moved away. Then, during his last illness, things had gone from bad to worse.

At home, Paul became more and more tense, sitting silently in his father's study, answering Sarah sharply when she tried to ask questions.

He rose from the table one evening, leaving his meal half-finished.

'I'm not hungry.'

'But it's your favourite – steak pie,' his mother protested.

'Mother, I said I'm not hungry.'

As he shut the door behind him to spend another evening in the study, Grace sighed. She'd seen the light under his door and heard him pacing about, night after night.

'It was like this when he came back from the war,' she said despairingly to Sarah. 'I don't know what to do for the best.'

'You must leave it to him,' her daughter advised. 'It's Paul's life – we can't decide for him.'

Grace shook her head and rang for the maid to clear the table.

Soon, Paul knew, he had to decide. It wasn't fair to keep the workers guessing. It wasn't fair to leave all the managing of the farm to Jock. And it wasn't fair to keep Marian waiting for ever.

How could he ask her to share his life in the city, away from the farm and the fields and the countryside she knew? If she was unhappy, he would blame himself. And did she care enough for him to make such a drastic move? It would be too much to ask of her.

Perhaps she'd forget him after a while and settle down happily with someone else – maybe a farmer, or someone she'd known all her life…

Either way, he had to come to a decision.

A few days later, he knew he couldn't put it off any longer. He sat down at his desk.

Dear Marian…

No, that was too formal.

My dear Marian…

He began to write.

'I won't be long.' Marian picked up her basket, and wound her scarf round her neck. 'I'm just off to the village.'

She looked a little anxiously at Betsy. What could be wrong? Her mother went about her work almost mechanically these days, rarely humming her favourite old Scots airs. Even Robert's visit had made no difference.

Marian sighed. Perhaps Betsy would tell her in time.

'I've just a few things to do,' she went on.

Betsy nodded almost absentmindedly. After Marian had gone, she reached for the jars of currants and raisins. It was time to start preparing the fruit for the Christmas puddings, though she had little heart for celebrating this year.

The sun was low in the winter sky and, glancing out of the window, she noticed the berries on the rowan beside the door. It was going to be a hard winter. She must remember to put out food for the birds.

As she watched, a robin hopped on to the window-sill. Betsy smiled to herself and paused in her work.

She was so engrossed in her own thoughts, she wasn't aware of the first tentative tap at the door. And then there was a second knock, louder this time.

'That'll be Jess.' She brightened up. A visit from Jess was always a pleasure.

'Is that you, Jess? Come away in.'

But there was no answering greeting. Betsy was a little puzzled. Who would be calling at this time of day?

She wiped her hands on her apron.

'I'm just coming!' And she opened the door wide.

'What...? Where have you come from?' She took a step back, holding on to the door frame for support.

'I'm sorry. This must be a surprise for you.'

Betsy gazed in astonishment at Simone. Yes, it really was her, standing there clutching the hand of a small boy who looked up at Betsy with large, dark eyes.

'You'd … you'd better come in.' Betsy couldn't think of anything else to say. 'Don't stand there in the cold.'

Simone picked up her suitcase and pushed the little boy ahead of her.

'I didn't know you were coming.' Betsy couldn't take her eyes off Simone.

'I – did not know either,' the French girl replied haltingly. 'But I thought, it is nearly Christmas – *Noel,* we say – and I knew I must come back, if only to say I am sorry. I have hurt you very much.'

She stood facing Betsy and spoke in a rush, as if she had prepared her speech.

'I have done a great wrong, I know, and I would not expect you to forgive me. We – Pierre and I – we have not come to stay. I don't ask you to take me back, but … you were like a mother to me.' Her voice faltered.

'I don't know what to say.' Betsy stood, twisting a corner of her apron between her fingers. And then she noticed the little boy in his dark overcoat, a muffler wound around his neck, his feet clad in shabby old boots. Betsy's warm heart was touched.

'I expect you're a hungry little lad?' she asked.

He looked up at her, not understanding.

Simone translated quickly, and the dark eyes lit up.

Betsy knelt down and unwound the scarf and helped him off with his coat. She rubbed his cold hands between her own, and the boy gave her a slow, hesitant smile.

'I'll put the kettle on,' Betsy said briskly, rising.

At first Simone was wary, unsure of her welcome. But Betsy, intent on heaping up little Pierre's plate, responded, trying to make it easy for the girl.

At last she turned to Simone.

'I've regretted a lot of the things I said to you, Simone. I spoke sharply...'

'I deserved it,' the girl murmured.

'Maybe you did,' Betsy concurred, 'but we got on fine together, you and I.'

'Yes, you were always so kind to me.'

'So,' Betsy continued, 'we'll let bygones be bygones. I've wanted many times, to say I was sorry, too. And now...' Her eyes softened as she watched the little boy wiping his plate clean. 'When there's a bairn, it's different.'

'I'm back!' Marian, her arms full of parcels, pushed the door open. Then she paused in the doorway, and gave a cry of delight.

'Simone! Where did you come from? What a surprise! And this must be your little boy...'

Dropping her parcels on the table, she swept Simone into a warm embrace.

'Oh, it's so good to see you again!'

Simone burst into tears.

'How kind you are – both of you. I don't deserve such a welcome!'

'There...' Marian soothed her. 'Sit down and tell us everything that's happened...'

Slowly, Simone began to explain how she'd decided to bring Pierre back to Scotland.

'It's home to me,' she said softly.

'But we will not stay here,' she added quickly. 'I have the plans – I will work as a seamstress. I know I can find a post. And Pierre can go to school.'

'But for tonight,' Marian said firmly, 'you'll stay here. You can have Elspeth's room...'

'Who can have Elspeth's room?' There was a clatter at the back door as Elspeth took off her boots and flung down her bag.

'Simone! You're back! And who's this?'

'Pierre – my son.' Simone rose. 'Shake hands with Miss Elspeth,' she told him.

The small boy gave a formal little bow

before shaking hands.

'My, this is a surprise!' Elspeth's cheeks were flushed pink with the cold winter air. Looking at her, Betsy suddenly realised that her younger daughter was growing into a young woman.

'You've been away for *ages.*'Elspeth affected an admonishing tone. 'At least it seems like that!' She suddenly smiled. 'And we've so much to tell you! There's the sergeant and Bella getting married. And my scholarship – did you know about that? Simone, I've won a music scholarship!

'And Mr Holt – he's gone back to England, and no-one knows if he's coming back...'

Suddenly, Simone looked at Marian and saw the colour drain from her face.

'But what is this?' she said. 'Mr Holt...'

'Never mind about that for the moment,' Marian put in hastily. She couldn't bear to talk about Paul – not in front of everyone.

'What matters is that you're back,' she went on, 'and we're very glad to see you.'

She raised her cup.

'Welcome home, Simone.'

A fortnight before Christmas, the cottage was buzzing with excitement.

226

'I'm so glad you're here for the wedding,' Marian told Simone.

It was a crisp, clear December day, as Marian set off to walk to the manse. She'd helped Bella choose a new eggshell blue blouse for the wedding, to go with her Sunday navy blue costume. Betsy had insisted on lending the bride her own mother's pearl brooch.

'Something borrowed,' she'd reminded Bella. 'It'll bring you luck!'

'And you must have a poor-oot,' Jess had said.

'It's an old Scots custom,' Marian explained to Simone. 'The children crowd round the bridegroom when he leaves for the wedding, shouting "Poor-oot, poor-oot!" That means "pour-out", so he empties his pockets of pennies and halfpennies and throws the coins to the children.'

'I have never heard of such a custom!' Simone laughed.

'Oh, this will be a real Scots wedding,' Marian promised.

Jess had offered to cater for the reception, and it seemed half the village was there.

'What a feast!' Dougie's eyes opened wide as he gazed at the pies and sausage rolls and ham spread out on the table.

No-one had the heart to restrain him, today of all days, and Marian smiled as she saw him reach for yet another sausage roll.

'This is grand, eh, miss?' he beamed at her.

Later, as the guests gathered at the door to wave Bella and Jock off, Marian found herself thinking of Paul. If only he could have been here…

But she had little time to spare for her own thoughts. Term was nearly at an end.

For the meantime, Simone and Pierre were staying at the cottage. Betsy felt a new warmth in her heart as she looked at the little boy, and when he put his hand trustingly in hers, she felt as if he were her own grandson.

She enjoyed baking for him, tempting his appetite with bowls of creamy porridge, and teaching him some of the old rhymes she had taught her own children.

'Poor bairn,' she said to Jess. 'He's had a hard time of it.'

And then there was the school nativity play. Simone was busy making the angels' costumes, and Marian had enlisted the help of several mothers who were handy with a needle.

There was the end-of-term party, too.

Dougie followed Marian like a shadow, eager to carry books, or help with moving chairs and desks. He was growing taller, thriving in the clean fresh air of the country-side.

'My! There's a fair difference in our Dougie,' his mother, on a recent visit, had exclaimed to Marian.

Marian was pleased, but looking at the careworn little woman, she wondered how much chance the rest of her family might have, and longed to take them all under her care.

Now, however, she smiled, thinking of the football boots she'd bought for Dougie. And then she felt a sudden pang of loss – because it was Paul who had given her the money, just before he left.

'Buy a present for the boy – something he really wants,' he'd said.

'That means football boots!' Marian had laughed. 'That's the one thing he wants.'

How like Paul, she thought sadly. If only things had been different...

Somehow, Marian managed to cope with the end-of-term festivities. It was the first time the school had attempted a nativity play, and she was secretly a little proud.

No-one forget their lines; the angels

looked suitably angelic – it was hard to credit what trouble they'd been up to till now – and the closing strains of 'Still the Night' left more than one person with a lump in the throat.

After the school party, Marian had the time to help with Christmas preparations at home. Usually, it was a fairly quiet celebration with just the three of them.

'We must make it special for Pierre,' Betsy had said firmly. 'William's train set is still in the loft, Marian. Why don't you fetch it down? I'm sure Pierre would like to play with it.'

That was when Marian knew that Simone was forgiven and her mother had taken the little boy to her heart as if he were her own grandson.

Robert, too, recognised that Betsy was well on her way to recovery.

'You're looking much better,' he told her.

'I'm fine,' she told him cheerfully. 'And with a wee boy in the house, I've plenty to keep me busy.' She laid a hand on his arm.

'It's all right. You were kind, listening to my troubles. But Simone and I – we're friends again now.'

'I'm glad of that,' he told her warmly. As he set off on his rounds, he thought of

Simone. She was a brave woman; it must have taken courage to come back and face Betsy.

Robert had been deeply touched when Simone had entrusted her secret to him. The news that she was back in Blairgowrie gladdened his heart and he had admitted to himself that he hoped, one day, they could be more than friends.

She deserved someone who would care for her properly, and be a father to Pierre.

A few nights before Christmas, Marian wrapped the presents for Jess and Dougie. She couldn't wait to see Dougie on Christmas morning in the longed-for boots. There was a scarf Betsy had knitted for Jess, tobacco for Bob, and a tin of Jess's favourite tea.

She put the parcels into a basket and decided to walk up the lane to deliver them.

It was a clear evening and her footsteps echoed on the stony path as she made her way to the farm. The stars seemed specially bright tonight.

When she reached the farmhouse, she was surprised to see that there were lights on. Jess must have decided to stay late, perhaps to do a spot of extra cleaning, or some baking. Marian quickened her pace, looking forward to the warmth of her kitchen.

'Jess! Are you in?' Marian put her head round the kitchen door, but to her surprise, there was no-one there – no warm, comforting smell of ironed sheets or the rich aroma of newly baked fruit cake.

The big table was scrubbed, the tea towels hung on the pulley to dry, and the hearth was swept and clean. But there was no sign of Jess.

Marian was a little puzzled, but then she saw the light under the study door. Jess must be upstairs. Marian left her basket on the kitchen table and climbed the stairs.

'Jess – it's Marian...'

She pushed open the door of the study and gasped. Oh, no, it wasn't – it was impossible!

Once before, she had opened the door to find a figure seated in her father's chair. Then, she'd had a foolish momentary fancy that it was her father...

She blinked rapidly and steadied herself by clutching the door handle.

'Marian.'

The tall figure rose from the chair.

'Paul!' Marian found herself shaking. 'I thought ... my father's chair.'

'Did I startle you?'

'You did, rather.' Marian gave a nervous little laugh. 'But why – I mean, what are you doing here?'

'I came to see you.'

'Me?'

'I wrote a rather stupid letter – you must have thought me pretty cold and unfeeling... You see, when I wrote it, I thought I'd no choice. I thought I had to take over the business...'

Marian said nothing, but continued to gaze at him.

'But a lot's happened since then. So I thought I'd come back to see you.'

Still Marian said nothing, but it seemed as if her heart began to beat faster.

'But I didn't expect to see you tonight...' He gave a little smile. 'So I haven't any fine speeches prepared. I'm not much of a one for fine speeches anyway.'

He crossed the room and took her hands in his.

'When I wrote, I had nothing to offer you – I couldn't ask you to leave your home and family and live in a city in all the noise and dirt and soot, after this...'

'As if that mattered,' Marian said so softly that he could hardly hear her.

'You mean...?' He put his arms round her

233

and she looked up at him.

'To think I nearly lost you,' he said. 'I love you, Marian, but I couldn't ask you to change your life, just for me.'

'Just for you...' Marian mocked gently. 'Paul, I wouldn't care where I lived! As long as it was with you.' She smiled up at him. 'I thought you'd forgotten all about me.'

'As if I could. But, Marian, could you really love me? I know I'm stubborn...'

'So am I, remember?' She interrupted him with a smile.

'Yes, we've wasted quite enough time disagreeing.' He laughed. 'But now...'

He kissed her before she could say anything more.

'I can't believe this is happening,' Marian said. She looked up at him. 'You said things have changed. But I thought you were needed at home?'

'My family have been wonderful,' he explained. 'You see, my mother realised that I was only taking my father's place out of duty.' He smiled. 'She was quite fierce about it. "You'd be useless running the factory, when all the time you wanted to be a farmer", she told me.

'I said I'd give it a try, but she was adamant and told me it was time I did what

I really wanted to do. She said Father was proud of the success I've made of running the farm. I was glad of that. So she more or less told me to go away!'

'But the business?' Marian asked in concern. 'Who'll run it, if you don't?'

'Sarah!' He smiled. 'It seems she worked for Father before he became ill and learned a lot from him. She's been longing to get a chance to take over the reins. She'll be good at it, too. Sarah has a real head for business.

'We can go to visit them,' he went on in a rush. 'After Christmas, if you like, then we'll make plans – to live here always, on the berryfields of Blair. Oh, darling, I can't believe this is happening at long last...'

'I can't believe it, either.' Marian laughed, a little shakily. 'When I walked in here tonight, you were on my mind and then, there you were! Oh, Paul, I've missed you so much. But...' She hesitated. 'Are you sure? I mean...'

'Sure?' He held her more tightly. 'I've been sure since the first moment I saw you. Do you remember? You walked in here, into what was once your home.'

'I remember how I felt about *you*,' Marian said softly. 'But it's all so different now...'

The publishers hope that this book has given you enjoyable reading. Large Print Books are especially designed to be as easy to see and hold as possible. If you wish a complete list of our books please ask at your local library or write directly to:

Magna Large Print Books
Magna House, Long Preston,
Skipton, North Yorkshire.
BD23 4ND

This Large Print Book, for people
who cannot read normal print,
is published under the auspices of

THE ULVERSCROFT FOUNDATION

... we hope you have enjoyed this book.
Please think for a moment about those
who have worse eyesight than you ...
and are unable to even read or enjoy
Large Print without great difficulty.

You can help them by sending a
donation, large or small, to:

**The Ulverscroft Foundation,
1, The Green, Bradgate Road,
Anstey, Leicestershire, LE7 7FU,
England.**
or request a copy of our brochure for
more details.

The Foundation will use all donations
to assist those people who are visually
impaired and need special attention
with medical research, diagnosis
and treatment.

Thank you very much for your help.